RAINBOW END

Emma Callow is a successful career woman whose life is safe, rather dull and free of entanglements — except for her unexciting relationship with Dominic Trafford. Then she receives a letter which shakes her world and prompts her to take a 6,000-mile journey to find the father she can barely remember. Accompanied by the veterinary surgeon Nicholas Locke, she is plunged from a humdrum way of life into a world of adventure, danger and finally — tragedy . . .

HILDA ROTHWELL

◆

RAINBOW END

Complete and Unabridged

LINFORD
Leicester

First published in Great Britain in 1974 by
Robert Hale & Company, London

First Linford Edition
published 2008
by arrangement with
Robert Hale Limited, London

British Library CIP Data

Rothwell, Hilda
  Rainbow end.—Large print ed.—
  Linford romance library
  1. Fathers and daughters—Fiction 2. Family
  reunions—Fiction 3. Romantic suspense novels
  4. Large type books
  I. Title
  823.9'14 [F]

  ISBN 978–1–84782–454–7

Published by
F. A. Thorpe (Publishing)
Anstey, Leicestershire

Set by Words & Graphics Ltd.
Anstey, Leicestershire
Printed and bound in Great Britain by
T. J. International Ltd., Padstow, Cornwall

This book is printed on acid-free paper

To those two Samaritans, Morna and Derek K.,
B.V.M. & S., M.R.C.V.S.; B.V.M. & S., M.R.C.V.S.;
respectively.
With heartfelt gratitude for more kinds of
help than one.

H.R.

1

There was a girl at school whose father had been killed in the war when she was four. She was a few years older than myself, but I plucked up sufficient courage one day to ask her what she could remember about him.

He had apparently been something of a hero. At any rate, she was very proud of him and began to reel off some of his exploits in battle.

'No,' I remember saying. 'That's not what I mean. They're not things *you* remember. They're things you've been told.'

She was undoubtedly annoyed. She must have been a kindly girl at heart, however; or perhaps she saw how much it mattered to me.

'Well,' she said at last, reluctantly, 'I suppose I only remember one thing, really. I remember him sitting at the

1

breakfast table one morning. He was in uniform — I'm sure of that — and he took me on his knee and gave me the top off his breakfast egg. I must have been about three, I suppose. He seemed to be kissing me a lot. I don't really remember anything else.'

I nodded, and turned away. I had known, I think, how it would be. I remembered hearing my father's voice when I was four, and that was *all* I remembered about him.

But I know I was four because of the candles. They had decorated my birthday cake a few days earlier; one red, one green, one blue, and one yellow. I called them my rainbow candles, and in the way such things happen throughout one's life, they were destined to become one of those inexplicable landmarks that accumulate in the memory.

I loved them with my whole heart. Entranced by their vivid colours and delicately grooved sides, I had kept them after blowing them out and lain them tenderly in their tiny cardboard box, lined with cotton wool, to gloat over in bed at night. An only child (and, I suspect, a lonely one), it was the kind of solitary pleasure in which I was inclined to indulge.

I sat toying with them *that* night in the light of a banana-shaped moon that slanted through my window and across my bed. It *was* a bed, and not a cot. I was very tall for my age. Before falling asleep, however, I would secrete them in my own special hiding place, known to no one but me.

Perhaps because the moonlight was bright enough to lend my candles some semblance of ethereal colour, the sound of my father's voice that night remains inextricably mingled with the sight and feel of them.

He seemed to be shouting, though this may not have been so. It was, I now realise, the kind of house in which sound would travel only too clearly. I often tapped my wall to hear the hollow thud so produced, and the faint vertical ridges visible beneath the yellow colour wash made it clear to me in later years that the entire structure must have been made of wood.

The house was built on one level, so that his voice came to me from the tiny hall, not ten paces from my door. And yet, he was a quiet man, and I had never heard him speak so loudly before.

He repeated himself, too, again and again, discussing, it seemed, someone named Jim Stone, whom he appeared to be defending against my mother's fiercely whispered: 'You fool. You utter *fool*.' And then the voices ceased abruptly. There was the hollow, boxy sound of wood on wood as the front door slammed, followed by complete silence.

It terrified me, I remember; that silence. I listened for a while, far too afraid to leave my room for reassurance that one of them at least remained and I was not alone, in case it was not so. In the end, I laid my candles in their box, buried my face in the pillow, pulled the light, thin bedcovers over my head, and,

I suppose, fell asleep.

After that, there was no more Daddy. Just my mother, quiet-voiced and authoritative, packing cases and mopping my tears as she prised one battered, beloved toy after another from my tenacious fingers. For I was a hoarder (unlike my mother, who was, I think I considered even then, all too ready to instruct me to 'throw that rubbish away').

'No, Emma. You can't take it. No, nor that. And what's this? Oh, *Emma*. Candles, of all things. They can't be used again. See, the wicks are all burnt, and you've squeezed them out of shape. Throw them away. Look, here's Delia. You may take her.'

I think it was Delia; or Dahlia perhaps. A doll I hated. Dainty and curvaceous and coyly simpering; all the things that I was not.

'For heaven's sake, don't start crying again. There isn't time. Anyway, you're too *big* to cry. Tall girls look ridiculous crying. It's something you'd better

5

remember, because you grow more like your father every day.'

That was all I ever remembered, really, apart from a hotch-potch of vague impressions; scurrying movement alternating with endless periods of boring inactivity, and the churning of ink-blue, foam-capped water far below what must, of course, have been the deck of a ship.

2

I let myself into my flat with one hand, shoulder bag pressed against my side, a brown paper bag of groceries balanced on my other arm. The envelope lay on the mat just inside, the flap side uppermost; no more than an anonymous pale rectangle in the dark hallway.

I was in no position to pick it up just then, so I elbowed the door shut behind me and went straight through into the tiny kitchen, lowering my bag first, with a disgusted glance at the strap. The stitching was inside the wretched thing, between leather and lining; how could I have known it was about to give?

It was late, and I was hungry. It was one thing attaining the plum position of personal secretary to Mr Mostyn, the salary and perks being not inconsiderable. It was quite another living up to it. While pert, pretty young things, fresh from their commercial colleges, clattered happily out of the office in their knee-length boots and swinging skirts dead on the stroke of five, I sat waiting for the great man to finish his call to Birmingham so that he could begin dictating the 'one or two urgent letters' that could never, it seemed, wait until tomorrow, however late it was.

I emptied my groceries on to the counter, slid a couple of lamb chops under the grill, and poured myself a sherry. At least it was Friday. I sat down on my one and only kitchen chair and put up a hand to the thick coil of hair that lay so heavily upon my neck. No wonder my head ached. I began desultorily pulling out the pins and massaging my nape and shoulders wearily. My hair was too thick; too heavy to be carried on the top of my spine throughout a long and busy day. This time I would have at least six inches lopped off. When I next went home —

I remembered again that it was

Friday, and found the thought not quite so cheering this time. At any moment now the telephone would ring, and my mother's flutelike voice would be asking me why I had not caught the train straight from the office to spend my weekend at home; why I had not gone down the weekend before; or the weekend before that —

Heavens, it must be at least a month. I should have to agree to go tomorrow, without a doubt. For one thing, I was beginning to run out of excuses. For another, I was feeling particularly lonely and low in spirits for some unaccountable reason; anyway, it would be nice to see my harebrained young brother Brian again.

I turned the chops, buttered a roll, and set out apples and cheese. The telephone had still not rung by the time my meal was ready and I fell upon it thankfully, pouring another sherry with an air of grim abandon because if I did have a weekend looming up I might just as well do something to celebrate the fact.

I had almost finished washing up when the telephone rang. I dried my hands, not hurrying, and wandered out of the kitchen and across the small hall into the living room. Something white, lying in the shadows by the door, caught my eye, but not my memory. Must have dropped something coming in, I thought as I reached for the receiver.

'*Emma.*' Nobody — but nobody — said 'Emma' the way my mother did. There was the faintest of accusatory tones, as always, almost as though she could see the unaccustomed colour on my pale, bony cheeks and had guessed about the second glass of sherry, or as though she were astonished to find me there at all, instead of whooping it up on the town with my elderly (and happily married) boss. Or —

No; impossibe to define, really. After all, she couldn't see me and I *was* always there when she rang, and that faint note of disapproval was never absent, whether from the other end of a telephone or not. Now when she addressed Brian —

'*Emma*.'

'Yes, Mother. How are you?' She said 'Brian' on a different note entirely —

'So Allan suggested that I pop along to Doctor Trafford. However, I have never believed in coddling myself.' A pause.

'No, Mother, I know.' There was a special tone for Allan, too, as her husband and head of the family.

' — but then at the Askew's bridge party I felt it again, only much worse.'

What? I wondered desperately. This was the invariable consequence of asking Mother how she was. Now forty-nine or so, she was still attractive, slim, and petite, and had never known a day's real illness that I could recall throughout the twenty-nine years of my life.

'So I said to Doctor Trafford — '

'Oh? So you did go to see him?'

'Why don't you *listen*, Emma? I told

you I met him in Barkers' when I went for the liniment.'

'Yes. Of course.'

A bad back, perhaps? Or a strained wrist? Or had Brian sustained some sporting injury? I knew better than to ask again, however.

' — looking his age these days. I remarked how wonderful it must be now that Dominic is qualified.'

'He's been qualified for over a year, Mother.' Dominic was Doctor Trafford's son.

'You know what I mean. All this houseman nonsense. Now he's home helping his father as he should. I thought perhaps if you came down tomorrow we could ask them round for a drink after church on Sunday.'

'Yes, Mother.' I grinned wryly into the telephone. Mother had been trying to get me paired off with Dominic for years. But poor Dominic could not, I suspected, come to terms with his five foot nine as against my five foot ten; though if it came to that, I had never been able to come to terms with it myself.

'You *are* coming tomorrow?' The slight uncertainty in her voice surprised me, and in some absurd way lifted my spirits. She had, then, been half-prepared for my refusal. She was not, it seemed, as sure of me as she would have me believe.

'I'll come. Not too early though. I worked late this evening and I may sleep in a bit. I'll catch the later train — see you about twelve.'

'Allan can pick you up, then. He's popping into the office for an hour but he'll be through by then.'

I put the phone down at last, bemused by the sudden solicitude, and instead of going back to the kitchen, sank into an armchair, laying my head wearily against the cushion. My hair hung about my back and shoulders, reminding me of the girls of my brother's generation; of Brian's dolly birds and the chattering little covey at the office, turning their heads from side to side with coltlike but contrived movements so that the curtains of shining hair could fall about their round, smooth young faces and they could scoop it back in order to peer up at me. 'Yes, Miss Callow. No, Miss Callow. I'm sorry, Miss Callow.' I was beginning to understand what was meant by the generation gap; was already feeling the first chill draught blowing in my direction. And I had not, as yet, even begun to live.

I picked up a handful of hair and stared at it. I should have asked Mother to book me in at her hairdresser's for tomorrow. Corn blond, Mother's hairdresser called it.

'*Lovely* hair you have, Miss Callow, if I may say so. So thick, and such a lovely colour.'

Well, that was something, I supposed. Not much, of course, these days, when one considered that if one's hair was *not* a lovely colour one could soon make it so, and if it were not thick enough one could always reinforce it with a wig. But something, all the same.

The living room door gave on to the single bedroom, and on an impulse I went through and across to the dressing table. A pair of scissors lay on the tallboy and I picked them up. Six inches. Well, I could lop that off myself. Less weight on my neck for the weekend.

I began to cut, watching the thick, stubborn stuff as it slid irritatingly away from the blades, and filled with a sudden absurd sense of dismay as I realised that what I had begun, I should now have to finish.

Of course it took far longer than I had expected, and I ended up, by the time I had got the ends reasonably level, with an agonising ache in my arms, and shoulder-length hair, which was not at all what I had intended.

Wearily I switched off the lights in the kitchen and living room, brushed my teeth, and climbed into bed. It was indeed a tame and blameless life I lived; but then, there seemed neither time nor opportunity for anything else. I was surely destined, as my mother so desperately — and so obviously — feared, for the shelf, the role of aunt to my half-brother's children as time went by, and a dedicated career-woman existence, leading to a prim and dessicated old age.

As I switched off my bedside light, far too exhausted to read, I smiled to myself drowsily. There *was* the matter of the two sherries. Perhaps I should take to solitary drinking as time went by.

Sometime during the night, quite without reason as far as I know, I awoke from a deep sleep and remembered the letter. I saw it, in my mind's eye, as clearly as though I were looking down at it all over again, pale and enigmatic on the mat.

A bill? But I never got bills, apart from the gas and electricity. Anyway, the flap was sealed. Wasn't it?

I found that I was not sure about this either way, and sleep intervened before I had the matter clear in my mind. But the thought must have remained with me, because I woke at a ridiculously early hour with a sense of urgency that prodded me from my warm, comfortable bed and out into the hallway.

I picked up the letter, yawning and turning it over in my hand while I wandered into the kitchen to switch on the kettle. They were quite the prettiest and most colourful stamps I had ever seen. A zebra, stark black-and-white against an apricot sky, decorated one. The other appeared to consist of a background of lush green forest, with three of four gazelle-like creatures leaping effortlessly across the scene.

The word *impala* came quite unbidden to my mind. They were impala, some monitor in my brain assured me; no possible doubt about it. The address was typewritten, the postmark quite illegible against the vivid background of the stamps.

As I opened the kitchen drawer in search of a knife to slit open the envelope, the kettle boiled, and I reached for the teapot and caddy instead.

I was mildly intrigued, as much by the word impala as by anything else. So much so that, leaving the tea to draw, I crossed the hall to the living room and picked up the battered *Concise Oxford* that had travelled with me through boarding school. The dark-blue cover was scored and scratched, and the spine had been painstakingly scotch-taped into position many times, but there were no pages missing; I was sure of that.

I poured my tea and flicked to the I's. IMPACT, IMPAIR, IMPALE, IMPALPABLE —

That was odd. There appeared to be no such word. Besides, now that I thought about it, I could not remember ever having heard it before. Where could I have got it from?

I reached for the kitchen knife and slit the envelope, eyeing the stamps thoughtfully. African, without a doubt, with all that luxuriant greenery and the zebra and impala —

I shook my head impatiently and pulled out the single sheet of flimsy notepaper the envelope contained. I knew nobody in Africa; nobody at all. There had been the girl who left the office to go out there on some voluntary mission for a year, but that was at least three years ago, and we had never corresponded, anyway.

'Lowell and Driscoll,' I read. 'Solicitors; Commissioners for Oaths. Stanley Buildings, Stanley Avenue, CHUNDI, MINZANDA.'

'Dear Madam — '

My tea grew cold; so did my feet, while I stared down at the typescript; first with incredulity, then with a sense of intolerable sadness and loss, and finally with a burning anger such as I had never known.

Aeons later, or so it seemed, I refilled and plugged in the kettle, this time gulping the tea avidly the moment it was made. I picked up the dictionary and put it back where it belonged, remembering as I did so those lonely

19

years at boarding school just before, and after, my mother's marriage to Allan Hammond, and the equally lonely visits home to Fleetchurch for the holidays, watching, as one looking through glass, the utter completeness of a happy marriage in which I was an intruder.

The arrival of Brian had, it seemed, pushed me finally beyond the pale. I was nearly eleven when Brian was born, well into my second year at boarding school, and becoming already as resigned as I could ever be to my nickname of Lofty. I had hoped, then, that they would bring me home to help with my baby brother, and had been pleased, if anything, by his arrival. I could not have been more wrong.

And yet my stepfather was kind enough, I suppose; my brother a normal, decent boy. But the age gap was too great for there to be any real companionship, and my mother had never, even before the advent of Allan on the scene, become reconciled to the *kind* of daughter she had produced. 'You grow more like your father every day.'

Skipping breakfast — I could not have eaten had my life depended upon it — I bathed and dressed rapidly, twisting my shorn hair into a loose roll, and washed up my teacup. Fragments of childhood memories flitted in and out of my mind as I moved about, making my bed, straightening the cushions, applying make-up —

There was the time when my mother had taken my hand — I was about nine — to cross the busy Fleetchurch High Street, only to discover for the first time, and with a distaste she could not conceal, that my hand was fractionally larger than her own, so that my long fingers curled around the backs of hers. She had never taken my hand again from that day on; my arm, or my elbow, perhaps. Never my hand.

I caught the earlier train with minutes to spare. There was the usual Saturday crowd at Victoria and I was lucky to find a seat, but at least the chatter of the two or three couples in the compartment kept me from thinking, impossible as I have always found it to travel alone in a train without listening to the snippets of conversation around me (wondering precisely what it was that the bowler-hatted man's wife *did* at the previous evening's drinks party to make him so incensed).

I crossed over the footbridge at Fleetchurch station and hesitated as my stepfather's office building came into view at the corner of the High Street. Allan Hammond and Partners; Estate Agents; Surveyors; Valuers; Management Developers; was inscribed in gold lettering across the plate-glass windows.

I had a sudden, almost irresistible longing to talk to somebody about the letter that lay in my handbag before confronting my mother. Someone detached, as it were. Heaven knew, Allan had always been that. A well-groomed, stocky man of about my own height (height invariably entered into my judgments of people;

especially men); good-looking in a President Nixonish sort of way, smoothly sophisticated and — detached.

But he *was* her husband. I hurried on instead, passing the taxi rank so that I was away from the High Street and halfway across the park before I realised that I had given myself an uphill walk with the encumbrance of an overnight case as well as a handbag and umbrella. But at least it was not raining.

There was no sign of Brian's runabout in the drive, but my mother's green Anglia stood in its usual place in the double car-port at the side of the house. Not until I saw it did it occur to me that she might have been out. She was not, after all, expecting me until midday.

She must have seen me from a window, because as I walked up the short, wide drive with its neat, narrow borders of autumn flowers, she appeared at the front door.

My mother always managed to greet me while retaining a faint crease between her brows, as though I were an exasperating domestic animal of whom she was reasonably fond, or an indelible scratch upon an otherwise quite serviceable pair of shoes.

'Emma. Now why on earth didn't you ring and *say* you were catching the earlier train after all?' She leaned forward to brush my cheek with her lips before I stepped up on to her level, as it were. 'Really — !'

'I didn't see that it mattered.'

'But I might have been out.'

'I have a key.'

'But — but — ' I put down my case and followed her through the hall and into the wide, attractive living room that looked out on to the front of the house, waiting patiently while she sought for some further objection to my earlier arrival, and never doubting that she would find one.

I sat down, trying to imagine as I drew off my gloves what it would have been like to have her fling the door wide and cry: '*Emma*! You caught the early train after all. How lovely, darling. And how wonderful to see you.'

I think I grinned faintly at this flight of imagination, and it must have shown. At any rate it gave her her cue. 'Then there's Allan. I do think you might *consider* people more, Emma. You always were a law to yourself. There he is, expecting you to call in at the office, so that he can drive you home — '

'Wasn't he going in anyway?'

'That's not the point.'

'*Mother.*'

'Besides, he'll probably wait for you now.'

I crossed over to the telephone table by the door, picked up the receiver and dialled my stepfather's number. As I expected, he answered himself; there would be no staff around on a Saturday.

'Allan? Emma here. I'm — Yes, thanks. Fine. I'm at home. I caught — Oh, well. You know how it is when you plan to sleep in. Right. Just wanted to let you know. 'Bye.'

I turned to find my mother eyeing me

uncertainly, and recalled my intuitive guess of the previous evening; that she was not as sure of me as she liked to think.

I sat down again, forcing myself to lean back, and crossing one long leg over the other.

She hesitated, then perched herself on the edge of a thoroughly uncomfortable 'occasional' chair, pressing her knees and ankles firmly together, her eyes travelling along my legs from ankle to knee with barely concealed envy. Mother's legs were her only poor feature. I reached for my handbag, placed it on my knee and opened it, while the silence grew.

'Emma,' said my mother at last. 'Is something — ?' She stopped, quite suddenly, as I drew out the envelope, flap side towards me, holding it so that the stamps faced her. She stared at them, fascinated.

'Pretty, aren't they?' I leaned towards her, showing her more clearly. 'African, of course. Some place called Minzanda, if I remember aright. Zebra and — impala, wouldn't you say?'

'I don't — ' Her throat was working so that, for a moment, her well-cared-for neck looked almost old, and in that moment the anger I had nursed so carefully for just this moment began to seep away. I slipped from my chair to kneel beside her, hating the lump that rose in my throat at her distress. I had a right to be angry, after all, while her distress was of her own making.

'Mother.' I held her eyes with my own. Indeed, I am certain that at that moment she could not have looked away.

'Mother. Why did you never tell me that my father was alive? Why have you let me believe, all these years, that he was dead? And why — why have you never talked to me about him?'

3

It must have been a full minute before she found her voice; long enough for me to realise that she was in fact in a state of shock.

I am not, I suppose, by nature a belligerent type (too cold, my mother would say), and as I poured a little of my stepfather's best brandy into a glass and held it to her lips I felt all the old diffidence creeping back inside me.

'He — he wrote to you?'

I shook my head. 'Another sip — come on. I'm — ' I stopped myself, just in time, from saying, 'I'm sorry I upset you.' Not this time. If there was any apologising to be done, it must come from her. But I found I could not harass my own mother, nor suppress a sense of guilt at the sight of her white face.

I was taking the glass from her when

Allan's car entered the drive. Through the window I saw him open the rear door and lift his bulging briefcase from the back seat, wind up the windows and turn towards the house, sorting the door key from the bunch in his hand as he approached.

I looked at my mother again, and was unable to suppress a smile. The extent of her recovery was remarkable; far greater than the brandy could have produced. Her head was high, some of the colour had returned to her cheeks, and the glint in her beautiful grey-green eyes as they met mine was unmistakable. Now, they seemed to be saying, you will have my husband to deal with instead of a small, fragile woman half your size.

The front door opened and closed, there was the slap of leather against wood as Allan placed his briefcase on the hallstand, and he strode into the room.

'Emma.' He dropped a kiss in the region of my chin. 'Nice to see you.' He bent to kiss my mother, paused midway, studied her, and straightened.

'Something wrong?' He was asking the question of me. The genial half-smile had faded.

'Where's Brian?' My mother's voice was almost back to its normal dulcet tones. She never raised it; she never had to.

Allan bent towards her again. Their lips met in what was far more than a cursory kiss. A flicker of envy arose in me for a moment. How wonderful it must be —

'With some girl or other. He'll be home for lunch. Barbara, something's wrong. What *is* it, dear?'

He straightened and shot me a puzzled, half-humorous look. 'Have you two women been having words, or something?'

The letter was still in my hand. Silently I held it out to him, my eyes on his face. My mother put out a hand as though in protest.

For once, however, Allan ignored her. The flimsy paper crackled in the silence as he unfolded it and began to mutter:

'Lowell and Driscoll — Never heard of 'em. Mizanda? Where have I heard that name before?'

Then he caught my eye and had the grace to blush. He turned to my mother. 'Barbara, have you read this?'

She shook her head, moistening her lips as though she wanted to say something. Again the words would not seem to come.

'But — ' He flicked the envelope over. 'Who's it to? Oh, you.' He looked at me then, frowning.

'When did you get this?'

'Now. This weekend. Read it, please.'

'But how could they possibly know your address? Minzanda, Minzanda. Isn't that one of those tinpot African states someone or other keeps on inventing? Can't keep track of 'em myself.' He paused uncertainly, as his eyes met Mother's. He doesn't know whether to admit that he knows, I thought.

'Read it.'

He gave my mother another brief

glance, and began to read aloud:

'*Dear Madam,*

Acting upon instructions from our client, Mr Nicholas Richard Locke, of Chundi, we have been for some time past engaged in discovering the whereabouts of one Emma Jane Callow, only daughter of Andrew Grant Callow, and his former wife Barbara, née Bennett.

'*It would appear from our enquiries that you are the lady in question, and we are requested by our client to ask you to advise us whether this is so. Perhaps in so doing you will furnish us with proof of identity in the form of certified copies of your parents' marriage certificate and your birth certificate.*

'*In view of the lapse of time due to tracing your whereabouts, our client would be grateful if the matter could be treated as being of some urgency.*

Yours faithfully,

Jerome Driscoll.'

'He's dead. He must be dead. You said he was alive.' As I turned and looked at her, my mother pressed her fingers over her mouth while her eyes flickered from me towards Allan and back again.

'Sounds like it.' Allan folded the letter, replaced it meticulously in the envelope, and handed it to me. His face wore the apprehensive expression of a man who sees himself getting involved with something that is no concern of his, that he would far rather pass by, but does not quite — as yet — see how he decently can.

'You — you said he was alive.' She was accusing me; putting me in the wrong for giving her an unncessary shock.

'Why does it matter to you so much? In any case, that wasn't what I meant, and you know it. If — if my father *is* dead, it can be only recently. Yet all these years you've led me to believe he died when I was small — that you were a widow when you married Allan.

33

You've been lying to me all my life — '

'Emma.' Allan put out a hand as though to draw me towards him. I moved away, out of reach.

'You too. You knew too, didn't you?'

He hesitated, then nodded. 'Yes, I knew. I knew that your mother divorced your father for desertion when you were seven. For *desertion*, Emma; and she wanted you to grow up believing him to have died.'

'But why? *Why?*'

He moved his shoulders uneasily. 'We thought it would be best.'

'And who were you to judge?'

'Someone had to; you were too young. My dear girl, someone always has to make the decisions for children, as you'll find out for yourself one day, no doubt.'

'I'm not a child now. I haven't been one for a very long time. At what age did you both — decide — I'd be old enough to be told the truth about my own father?'

'Emma, listen to me.' He patted his

pockets for cigarettes, glanced irritably about him, and strode towards the box on the mantelpiece. I waited, watching him light it, draw upon it, and lean back against the mantel with both arms outstretched.

'Your father treated your mother abominably. You, too, if you think about it. He walked out on her — literally walked away one night — and never came back.'

'Where? Where was this? Somewhere in Africa?'

He looked a little surprised, glanced down at my mother briefly, then back at me.

'Come, my dear. You were very young, it's true, but surely you remember coming home? Coming back to Fleetchurch with your mother, to live with your grandparents?'

'I remember my grandparents perfectly well. I remember Grandma dying, then Grandpa. And I remember — ' I frowned, trying to sort out the jumble of babyhood memories that were all I had left of those far-off days. 'A ship, I think. Was it — did we come on a ship?'

My mother gave a single, brief nod. 'From Cape Town.'

'But I was born in Fleetchurch. My birth certificate says so.'

'We left England just after your third birthday to join him. I met your father during the war. We were married within two months, and you — you were on the way within weeks of the wedding.'

She was quite calm now, gazing ahead as though trying to recapture that time, laced fingers lying in her lap.

'He said it was too hot; not suitable for a small child, and that the medical facilities — Too *hot*! Dear God.' She began to laugh, then covered her face with her hands. Two strides brought Allan to her side. He dropped to his knees and took her hands in his, rubbing and caressing them gently.

'Barbara darling.' He spared a second to shoot a look of accusation in my direction.

'I was nineteen. *Nineteen.*' My mother stared at me over Allan's head. 'Ten years younger than you are now. D'you remember being nineteen, Emma? All the silly, grandiose, romantic dreams — ? Oh, what's the use? You've always been more his daughter than mine, though heaven knows why, when you can't even remember him.'

'What was he like? Was he English?'

'You could say so. British, anyway. He was born in Northern Rhodesia, of an English father and a Scots mother.' She gave me a purely feminine, and faintly malicious, glance. 'That's where your boniness comes from, no doubt. The Scots are inclined to be angular, don't you find?'

I ignored this.

'And you went — we — went there? But that's Zambia now. Isn't it?'

'Yes, yes. No, we didn't go there. I've never been there. There was this protectorate, Minzanda, needing field officers. He'd been brought up in Africa; he missed it. He was over here on leave when war broke out, so he joined up as a matter of course.'

'My grandparents. What happened to them?'

'His father was already retired from the Colonial Service. I believe they settled in Southern Rhodesia, as it was called then. But they were oldish; in their sixties before the war. They'll be long dead. He was the only child.'

'Did you ever meet them?'

'Yes, once. He took me to Salisbury especially. I thought he'd taken me to Paradise, after that — that terrible place —'

'Was I there? Was I with you? Did they see me?' I found myself gripping my hands together so tightly that the palms were moist. Surely someone, somewhere, had loved the baby girl that I had been; delighted in her; been thrilled that she was alive?

'Yes. They'd hoped for a boy, of course, Andrew being their only son. But they thought you were very sweet. I remember they said there was plenty of time.'

I stood, silent and bitter, looking down at them both, and turning over in my mind my mother's reply.

The silence was shattered by the din of Brian's jalopy entering the drive. There was a banging of doors so ferocious that I turned my head in half-expectation of seeing the vehicle disintegrate before my eyes. He climbed out, whistling, and sauntered towards the house. There was the click of his key in the latch, a slam as he thrust the door shut, and in he came.

He was a good-looking boy; no doubt about it. He grinned as he saw me, stepped towards me with lightning rapidity, and flicked a hand behind my head in a time-honoured trick of his. He had always delighted in pulling every hairpin out of my head in a shorter time than it took me to stop him. Usually, these days, I had the better of him. But not this time; it was too short to offer much resistance.

He stood, hairpins in hand, looking as surprised at his success as I was myself. I had completely forgotten my hair-lopping efforts of the previous evening.

'Good Lord. You've had it cut. Well, well.' He was rather fond of saying 'Well, well,' on a supercilious note, at the moment.

'It was getting too heavy. Making my neck ache. But I cut too much off, I think.'

He studied me for a moment, running a hand through his longish black hair. He had inherited my mother's eyes — so, for that matter, had I — and his were level with my own as our glances met. There was a speculative look in them as he weighed me up, then he flicked his fingers.

'Got it.' The look changed to something almost appreciative. 'That old bird — what's her name? Saw a film of hers on telly a couple of weeks back. Oh, you know. Garbo. That's the one. You look just like her, cheekbones and all.' He flicked a hand at me as he turned away.

'Hi, Mum. Hello, Dad. Must just have a wash. What's for lunch? I'm starving.' He reached the door, shot me an amused glance, and said: 'You ought to keep it like that. Suits you.' As he disappeared into the hall I heard him mutter: 'Greta Garbo. That's the one. Well, *well*.' His head shot round the door again, and he winked back at me.

'Cheer up. They say she's got big feet, too.' He grinned and vanished once more.

* * *

There was no discussion regarding my father at the lunch table. Indeed, I could almost feel Mother and Allan willing me not to mention him. Allan and Brian had, it transpired, planned an afternoon's shooting at the Rifle Club, a favourite sport with them both. Allan was, in fact, a crack shot, with Brian improving rapidly with each afternoon's practice.

'Come with us, Emma?' Allan's eyes

rested upon me almost pleadingly. Clearly, he hoped to remove me from my mother's orbit until my temper cooled.

Brian gave a snort, then subsided as I shook my head. I looked at him in time to see him, pudding spoon upraised, cast his eyes to heaven as though in relief. Our eyes met, and he gave me a shamefaced grin.

'Well,' said Allan, obviously thinking furiously. 'There are a couple of things I have to see to first. You go on, Brian, when you've finished your lunch. I'll join you later.'

I helped my mother stack the dishwasher, waiting for her to speak. It appeared, however, that I had been sent to Coventry, a form of punishment she had practised upon me in childhood, and one she used still, if only in extremis, upon my brother.

The absurdity of it striking me suddenly, I leaned against the fridge where she was putting the luncheon remains away and said: 'What's the matter, Mother? Do you really believe that if you ignore my father's existence, and the arrival of that letter, the whole problem will simply go away?'

Even as I said it I found myself thinking: but that's exactly what she *has* done, for nearly a quarter of a century, and that's exactly what happened; it *did* go away; the whole thing. Except for me of course. And even I went away after a fashion. First to boarding school — something that had never even been mooted for my brother — and then to a life of my own in London. She had closed her eyes, so to speak, and it had gone away.

I felt the first stirrings of admiration for her. Such a small, fragile-seeming, softly spoken woman, and yet I had a strange intuitive conviction just then that she was stronger by far than my father had ever been. Somewhere inside me, I knew it for a fact.

Even now, Allan looked upon her as a lovely, delicate creature to be protected and cherished at all costs. But his was a strong personality, too, and he adored her; she had never needed to show her claws with him. Only with me. And with my father?

She put the butter carefully into the fridge and turned to face me.

'You talk of your father as though he were still alive, when every line of that letter proclaims his death.'

'It doesn't actually say so.'

'Oh, not in so many words, but that's what it means. In any case, he's been dead to me for twenty-five years.'

'For me, he's never even been alive. Can't you see, Mother, what you've done?'

'I can see that you're an ungrateful girl, who has never appreciated all that Allan has done for you.'

'That isn't true. I'm *fond* of Allan. He's always been kind to me. But let's be fair, Mother, I've cost him very little more than kindness. Grandpa did leave me all he had. Even Allan would agree — '

'Agree to what?' Allan stood in the doorway, looking from one to the other. He sighed.

'Oh, Lord. Are we at it again? Look, Emma. All you need to do is to write some sort of reply to this solicitor fellow, enclosing photostats of your birth certificate and so on as proof of identity, and the next move's with them. I'll draft it for you if you like.'

'No, thank you. I'm quite capable of writing a simple letter. Look, Allan. I'm sorry — I know you mean well. But with you it's Mother's interest that come first.'

'And so they should, young woman.'

'I'm not disputing it. It's just that in this, as in everything else, naturally you'll take her part. You're not even prepared to *listen* to me. Oh, can't you understand? For years I've believed my father was dead, and now suddenly I find he isn't — '

'Wasn't.'

'Wasn't, then.' I stopped, and stared at him. 'How do we know that? It doesn't say he's dead. He may be ill and needing — '

I stopped again, hearing my voice

begin to shake the way it always did whenever I allowed my feelings to show; something I seldom did, with Mother at any rate.

'They would have told you, Emma.' Allan's voice was gentle, almost compassionate. In comparison, my mother stood like a stone. I turned on her, feeling the anger build up in me again as it had when I first read Lowell and Driscoll's letter.

'You just don't care, do you? You don't care whether he's dead or alive. Or — or dying? A man you loved enough to marry, once, and have a child by. You've rubbed him out of your life just as you've rubbed him out of mine. Just as you'd have liked to rub *me* out, no doubt, and start all over with a brand new sheet.'

'Emma.' Allan's voice held its warning note.

'This is between my mother and me. Nothing, nothing at all to do with you, Allan.'

'By God, it is.' He actually began

moving up on me, hands clenched at his sides.

'No. I'm going to *make* her tell me about him. She's grown up you know, Allan, like me, and just as capable of looking after herself. She knows she's in the wrong about this.'

'Your father was no good, Emma. Listen to me and stop this ridiculous, melodramatic farce.' He was standing now within reaching distance; like Brian, his eyes were on a level with my own. But I could see the pleading look beneath the anger.

'Your mother acted for the best. We both did. He was no good — '

'How d'you know? Did you ever meet him?'

'Of course not. Don't be ridiculous.'

'Did you ever know anyone who did? Apart, of course, from his wife?' I looked at my mother again. Her face was very pale but she was quite composed in spite of Allan's anxiety.

'What I find so hard to forgive,' I told her, 'is that you have never told me a single thing about him in all these years, and that you have so little understanding that you can't even *see* that I had a right to know. That I've always longed to know, what's more. A girl can face not being able to remember her own father, but she has a right to be told what he was like.'

Her lip curled. 'What did he ever do for you to make you rush to his defence so nobly?'

'How can I possibly know? You've never told me. I don't even know who left whom, or why. I only know I'm not going to prejudge somebody as close to me as my own father on hearsay from one person,' I gestured towards Allan, 'and — and on hatred and prejudice from another.'

My mother recoiled as though my words and hurt her physically. 'Hatred and prejudice?'

'Yes. Did you think I never knew that you've been prejudiced even against me, your own daughter, all these years, simply because I remind you of him?'

For the first time my mother foresook the support of the counter she leaned against and came towards me. 'Emma, no. Don't say that — don't say that.' She put out a hand towards me gropingly, and I saw with amazement that her eyes were blind with tears. 'I tried so hard — so hard, all these years. I never dreamed — '

She began to sob, quietly, collapsing against me as though she were the child and I the mother. Allan moved past me as though to take her, but I put my arms around her and held her against my shoulder, trying to swallow the lump in my own throat as she whispered, again and again, between sobs: 'So sorry — I'm so sorry. I did try. I know I've loved you less than I should have done, but I *did* try not to let it show.'

Over her head, Allan's eyes met mine. There was a sort of shame lurking in them that brought the lump to my throat again, and I put out a hand to him.

'There's no need to look like that, Allan. I'm not your daughter after all, and I was old enough to know it when you married Mother. I think you've been as good a stepfather to me as anyone could hope for.'

The lines around his mouth relaxed. 'We've got on all right together, haven't we, Emma? On the whole?'

'Yes. Yes, indeed, of course we have. And you mustn't think — you must never think I'm not grateful.'

'Good. Good.' He leaned across and drew my mother towards him, pulling the handkerchief from his breast pocket to dry her tears.

'Come along now, darling. Mop up and smile. Emma's sorry she upset you. We can get this thing settled in no time at all. Emma will write her letter and that'll be that. Probably only want to notify her of his death; something of that sort. Now come along, no more crying. Emma didn't mean it.'

'Oh, yes I did. Oh, I didn't mean to upset you like this, Mother, but I did come here for a little plain speaking. Nobody should take away a child's knowledge of her own father the way you've both done — let her grow up believing him to be dead. Unless — ' I stopped, suddenly uncertain.

'I can understand,' I went on slowly, 'that in certain circumstances, perhaps — if one's father had been something quite terrible, like a murderer, that one might feel it better — '

I stopped again, waiting. Neither of them spoke. 'Mother, *was* my father some sort of criminal?'

She blew her nose with a somewhat brave-little-woman air of resolution. 'No, of course not. He — he was just obsessed, that's all.' She drew away from Allan, pulled a chair out from under the kitchen table, and sat down. We followed her, Allan holding my chair with an old-fashioned gallantry that would have amused me at any other time.

'Go on,' I said. 'Tell me about him. I really do intend to find out, you know.'

'He was a field officer, employed by the Government. Things in Africa were not what they are today. There were colonies and protectorates. Minzanda was a protectorate.' She frowned, then added: 'As a matter of fact, I don't think it's an independent state even now. I read something about it the other day in a newspaper article. They're too poor, or something. They have internal self-government, but are a very backward and poverty-stricken people, and they actually prefer the protection of Britain until they get on their feet, being landlocked and afraid of other states horning in.'

Allan laughed, trying, I thought, to lighten the atmosphere. 'Well, that's a change at any rate. Imagine anyone actually wanting poor old Britain these days.'

'The place was almost completely undeveloped. Prospecting was going on at a great rate, of course. Europeans of all races were always coming in from other territories, hoping to strike it rich with gold or copper or diamonds. Tin, too. There were a few tin mines opening up even then.'

She gave me a steady look. 'Your father got the prospecting bug. They get it badly you know, some of them. It's like gambling or drinking. He knew a fair amount about diamonds, I think; lots of people in those days were quite knowledgeable in an amateur kind of way. He used to trek out whenever he had time off. In the end,' she sniffed and mopped at her eyes again, 'he began wandering off in Government time as well.

'He was never *there*. I spent hours alone with you. His work took him miles away from Chundi as it was. When I protested he built a horrible little pole-and-dagga rondavel — that's a small round house of the type Africans build — on the prospecting site and took us with him.'

I stared at her, wide-eyed. 'Was it exciting? Did he find anything?'

'Oh, Emma. You just don't understand at all, do you? It was appalling. You can have no idea. He'd found Kimberlite, you see, or thought he had. Oh, dear, how can I — ? You know diamonds are found under certain volcanic conditions? A sort of chimney; a Kimberlite chimney. Even those discovered in river beds — alluvial diamonds — have been washed down from their original source —

'He couldn't leave it alone. He became morose and secretive. In the end he gave up his job, built a sort of frame house adjoining the rondavel, and took us out there to live. If one could call it living.'

She paused, smoothing her dishevelled hair into place. Allan, wearing his best estate agent's public relations manner, rose to fill the kettle at the sink and switch it on. He caught my eye and winked as he reached for cups and saucers.

'Good strong cuppa, that's what we all need.'

I smiled at him, feeling my eyes fill with tears. He was such a *good* sort, really. I was the odd man out in his marriage, not he, yet he had always striven for peace and goodwill, as far back as I could remember. The fact that I believed marriage should be for keeps, no matter what, was nothing to do with him. My father had — or so she said — deserted my mother long before he came on the scene; he had no hand in events in Minzanda.

And I was a grown woman, now, capable of earning my own living, and with Grandpa's legacy still intact. I had never needed to touch the capital, nor had Allan ever wished me to. All he wanted was for me to leave my mother in peace.

Perhaps she was right, anyway, I reflected, sipping my tea, and only half-listening while she and Allan conversed determinedly upon anything but Africa. Perhaps she *had* done the only thing possible in coming back to Fleetchurch and trying to forget my father. Perhaps she really *had* fled from a totally impossible situation. She could not have been more than twenty-four then. It must indeed have been an appalling situation for a young girl entirely alone, save for the company of a small child. None of this, to my mind, altered the fact that I had had a father all these years and she had never told me.

'Was there nobody else around? Nobody at all?'

They stared at me uncomprehendingly.

'Out there. Other prospectors, for instance, or their wives? This Mr Locke. Was he a prospector, or a field officer, or something? Do you remember him, Mother?'

She shook her head. 'Emma, all prospectors are a little odd — or they were then. Looking for the pot of gold — or whatever — at the end of the rainbow. They're solitary people, like your father. They *like* the bush, the heat, and the loneliness. They must, or they'd never do it. In the end they don't *need* companionship.'

She sipped her tea thoughtfully for a moment, then set her cup down in its saucer with a clatter. 'Look, I never want to talk about this again. It was a long time ago, and I've spent twenty-five years trying to forget it. I refuse to have it all resurrected again for you or anyone else.'

'What *is* a field officer?' I eyed her steadily.

'Oh! A hunter, basically.'

'A hunter? But I thought — I imagined a sort of district officer.'

'No. Let's drop it, Emma. Please. I've told you all I know — all that I can remember. Write your letter and leave it at that.'

I nodded, and said no more. But I think I had already made up my mind. All that remained was for me to see Mr Mostyn on Monday after I had sent a cable to Messrs. Lowell and Driscoll. If my father was alive I was going to find him; if he was dead, I would at least see, at first hand, how he had lived. Perhaps, too, there would be somebody, somewhere in Minzanda — this Mr Locke, for instance, or some other contemporary of his — who would talk to me about him without bias, and help me to get to know my own father. I knew that I should never rest now, until I had at least tried.

★ ★ ★

Mother's after-church drinks party on Sunday morning did nothing to weaken my resolve. Dominic, as I had expected, thought I was quite mad when I told him I was leaving for Africa as soon as possible.

'But what about your job?' He stared at me in wonderment. 'You've already taken your holiday this year. Anyway, whoever heard of going off into the blue like that without finding out a little more about the country first? It's ridiculous, Emma.'

'The only way I know of to find out

anything about a country is to go there.'

His eyes travelled over my face and my loose, shoulder-length hair. 'Something's got into you,' he muttered, as though diagnosing some sort of undesirable bug.

'Indeed it has. And d'you know, I feel almost happy about it. Excited, anyway. By the way, can you squeeze me in for a smallpox vaccination tomorrow? Nice and early, before I leave for Town?'

I began to laugh at the expression on his face, which brought his father to the scene, asking to share the joke. After that it was a matter of minutes before everyone in the room became aware of my plans. Of them all, only Brian upheld me.

'Super idea,' he said enthusiastically. 'Wish I could come.' He caught my eye then, and grinned, adding with a discernment I had never credited him with: 'But that would spoil it, wouldn't it? Going alone's the whole point, I rather imagine. Wonder what it's like there in October? Weatherwise, that is.'

'Damned hot,' said old Doctor Trafford sourly. 'Hot and dry, I shouldn't wonder.' He frowned at me. 'Ruin your complexion, girl. Dry it up. Never heard such nonsense.' He walked away as though washing his hands of me entirely. I was not, he was probably thinking, a suitable wife for Dominic after all. As I had always suspected that Dominic did not wholeheartedly think so either, and I myself was quite sure of it, this idea did not come as such a severe blow as it might have done. At twenty-nine I had not only become used to my spinster 'shelf'; I was beginning, I suspected, to grow dangerously attached to it.

Thinking about it in the train the following morning, with Dominic's vaccine painlessly (so far) infiltrating my system, I realised that I had never been really in love with anyone since the age of twelve, when I developed a passion for the boy who delivered the newspapers at my boarding school. He was tall (which was bound to count with me), very dark, incredibly good-looking, and about fourteen.

I had thought of him incessantly during the whole of the summer holidays at home, comparing him with every boy I knew in Fleetchurch; wholly to their disadvantage, of course. I had been overjoyed when the holidays were over and I was able to peer from my dormitory window, as soon as I woke, for the term's first glimpse of him cycling along the drive with the satchel of newspapers slung across his shoulder.

I never saw him again. His successor was a ginger-haired stocky youth with freckles and a piercing whistle; from which time I wholeheartedly detested red hair and freckles, absurd as it may seem. As I had only glimpsed my loved one from a window, while he had never, as far as I knew, so much as set eyes upon me, it did not seem, in retrospect, to have been much of a love affair. For all that I suspected that he had remained in my memory as a sort of yardstick against which none of the occasional men in my life had measured up, so far.

On my arrival at the office I found myself with other things to think about. I had expected my interview with Mr Mostyn to be difficult, and that he might very well be rather cross at my announcement. In the event I could not even get through to him.

'Find your father?' he kept repeating. 'But how can you find him if he's dead? What's that? He *may* be alive? But surely, Miss Callow, you cannot seriously be contemplating throwing up an excellent position in my office to travel over six thousand miles to search for a man you can't remember, who has never tried to find *you*, who may or may not be alive, and who will be a complete stranger to you if you ever do find him? Surely not.'

In the end I had to leave it at that. I rather think he gained a vague impression, in the end, that my father was gravely ill and asking for me, and he begged me to return as soon as possible. Not that I deliberately set out to deceive him; I merely named the possibilities as they occurred to me, and this one patently appealed to him as being infinitely preferable to the reluctant conviction that he had been employing a lunatic as his personal assistant for the past three years.

4

As it was I did not leave for another week, having failed to take yellow fever and cholera into my calculations. I would need to be inoculated against both, I was assured, in order to enter Minzanda.

I had done very little flying; a trip to Paris and another to Rome were the sum total of my experiences to date. Both of which trips were so short as to be completely misleading, as I was soon to discover.

From London to Nairobi was straightforward enough; from Nairobi to Blantyre in Malawi very comfortable. It was at this point that the temperature first began to register, however. From Blantyre I flew on to Salisbury in Rhodesia, which my mother, I recalled, had described as 'a paradise after that dreadful place'. And as we circled the city, sparkling as though newly-washed in the crystal-clear air and golden sunshine, I imagined I could see what she meant until I remembered that she had been talking of a quarter of a century ago, or more, and that it must all be greatly changed.

At Salisbury I was put aboard a Dakota; the Chundi airstrip in Minzanda, I was informed kindly, being unable to accommodate anything larger.

I was, by this time, the only passenger attired in anything approaching formality. All the men wore shorts, the women loose cotton shifts, bare legs and sandals boasting a mere thong or two to keep them on. I had never felt so hot as I glanced down ruefully at my cream summer suit and silk blouse.

Everyone on board, it seemed, knew everyone else, so that the atmosphere was reminiscent of that of a village bus on its daily jaunt into the nearby market town. The woman beside me carried a cat basket in her lap; her sister-in-law had given her a kitten, she explained, but it needed 'seeing to'. She gave me the same friendly smile that she had bestowed on the man across the aisle with the broad-brimmed hat upon his lap, and mopped at her face with a large handkerchief.

'Is it always so hot?' I asked tentatively.

'Well, now.' She considered, smoothing her brown, freckled hands across the wicker basket as though to soothe the faintly mewing occupant. 'Salisbury's always cooler, you know. Being higher. Chundi, now, that's hot. Though not so hot as in the valley. But it is nearly the end of October, and you know what they call October in this part of Africa?'

I shook my head, and she laughed.

'Well, you'll soon know *why*, at any rate. Suicide month, that's what. Staying in Chundi, are you, love?'

'I — I don't know. Do you know Chundi? Is there a hotel where I could stay?'

'Know it? I live there, my dear. Well, there's Blake's I suppose.' She eyed me

66

dubiously. 'You'd be all right in the annexe I expect.' She hesitated. 'Did you bring some thinner clothes, love?'

I grinned. 'I thought these *were* thinner clothes. Yes, I've some cotton dresses. I expect I'll survive.'

She nodded, and turned her attention to the cat.

'Will you be able to get him — er — seen to? Is there a vet in Chundi?'

'Oh, Nick'll fix him for me. He's due in this weekend. Only gets in about once a month, you see.'

Gets in from where? I wondered, staring out of the window as the aircraft began to lose height. There was nothing below us; nothing at all, but parched golden-brown landscape, and an occasional scattering of tiny round buildings (the rondavels my mother had described, I supposed) as far as the eye could reach.

'Are we — are we coming in to land?'

She gave me an encouraging smile. 'Presently, love. Shan't be long now.'

I couldn't believe it. Somewhere in

the middle distance was a ridge, where a belt of green probably denoted trees and cultivation of a sort. I stared down as the plane passed over it, picking out a cluster of buildings among the trees.

'Chundi?' I pointed downwards.

She shook her head. 'That's the Bezuidenhout ranch. There's Chundi now, over there.'

I craned forward, unbelieving. I could see a single, incredibly short strip of metalled roadway, literally beginning and ending in the wilderness below, like a shot of an old Wild West ghost town. Cars moved along at intervals, disappearing into clouds of yellow dust as they reached the end or turned off between the few rows of widely spaced houses on either side of the tarmac.

We dipped again, more sharply, and I thought I could make out a handful of shop fronts edging the 'main' road. We circled briefly and then Chundi disappeared entirely as we came in to land on what must surely have been the only other strip of tarmac the place possessed. I saw the control tower, there was a faint thump as we touched down, and we slowed to a halt beside a cluster of single-storied, Nissen-type buildings whose red-painted galvanised roofs glistened in the sun like molten metal; and looked almost as hot.

Customs and Immigration formalities were anything but, so to speak. The same official, a middle-aged, leather-skinned man with a shock of grey hair and a peaked cap lying on the counter beside him, attended to both by the simple expedient of moving further along the counter after dealing with the last of us, while whiteclad Minzandan porters wheeled in our luggage.

As he knew most of the passengers, the greater part of the time was spent in conversations that consisted mainly of question and answer.

'Cooler in Salisbury, eh? What've you got there, Dora? Cat, eh? Well, now. Dora, man. You know that according to quarantine regulations — '

'It's very fit, Bob. Only wants seeing to. Nick'll be in this weekend. I'm going to ask him — '

'Nick, He's here now. Waiting for some samples off the plane. *Nick*! Yes, Miss.'

He beamed at me. 'Anything to declare? England, eh? What's it doing over there — snowing?'

I found myself smiling back, hot and exhausted as I was. 'Not quite, yet.'

He searched among the clutter on the counter for a stub of chalk and drew a cross vigorously on the pristine surface of my new case. 'I know. You've come for the sunshine.' He laughed hugely at his own joke as the male passengers passed handkerchiefs over their moist brows before replacing their wide-brimmed hats and preparing to depart, then looked up and over my shoulder. 'Ah, Nick. Dora's brought a cat in. What d'you think?'

Before I could move, a lean brown arm reached out over my shoulder, seized the cat basket and lifted it effortlessly over my head and out of sight.

Since no man I had met so far had ever been capable of such a feat, I didn't really believe it (though I had already noticed that almost every male I had encountered since the aircraft touched down was taller than I was, including the Customs — and Immigration — Officer) but I turned round to make sure, and encountered the tallest man I had ever seen.

He was busily engaged in removing the peg of the cat basket and studying the contents thoughtfully. Even with his head bent he was inches taller than anyone else; six foot three, I thought, or even four. He wore a khaki drill bush jacket and shorts, his incredibly long legs were bare, his feet encased — if one could call it that — in scuffed brown leather sandals. A down of dark hair lay across his forearms and the backs of his thin brown hands. His hair was dark brown, with touches of grey at the sides and brow. Unlike the other men, he did not appear to possess a hat.

'It's a lovely little thing, Nick, isn't it? Thank heaven it's your weekend in town. I was counting on it.'

He looked up quite suddenly, and I saw the flash of white teeth in an incredibly brown face as he grinned at her.

'Sweet talk'll get you nowhere,' he said. His voice, with its faintest of Scottish accents, surprised me. Had my Scottish grandmother sounded like that, I wondered wistfully, as my reason for being here began to fill my thoughts again?

'Tell you what. I'll take him home with me and give him a rabies jab for a start. Then we'll see. Eight miles out, your place, isn't it, Dora?'

'About that, yes.'

'Pretty safe, then. I'll keep him a while. Then we'll see.'

Town, I thought, panicking suddenly. But where *was* it? And how would I get there? During the past few minutes the sound of cars and vans, Land-Rovers and lorries had reached my ears, revving up and disappearing into the blue beyond the 'Airport' buildings, so that now there seemed to be hardly anyone left. But there must, surely, be a conveyance of some sort for visitors like myself. All the same, I'd better ask, before it was too late.

I turned towards Dora and whispered a little desperately: 'How far is it into Chundi? Shall I have to walk, or is there a bus or a taxi I could take?'

Her eyes widened at the word 'walk'. 'Three miles. 'Course you can't walk, love. What, in this heat? with that case to carry? It's kill you.' She was looking over my head, as the Customs Officer had done. 'I'll take you myself, come to that, dear, so don't get worried. Nobody's going to leave you here. But I live out quite a way, in the other direction, so we'll see if Nick — *Nick*.'

I turned sharply enough to almost cannon into him, thus causing him to notice me, I felt, for the first time. At any rate, notice me he did.

It was a very swift, head-to-toe glance that he gave me, but there was nothing in the least cursory about it. And as his gaze rested briefly upon the top of my head I was able, for the first time, to notice his eyes.

Of course, the tan must have had the effect of lightening their colour. Even so, they seemed an almost silvery-grey, the thick black brows jutting over them to give an even greater contrast in colour. There was that strange, almost bleached look about the black-ringed irises that one sees in men who have spent long periods at sea, or gazing out across wide expanses of snow; or, I supposed, unrelenting sunlit landscapes. They were the most arresting — and oddly attractive — eyes I had ever seen in a man.

They met mine for the merest fraction of a second as they flicked from the crown of my head, over my face, across my shoulders and down the length of my (by now slightly wilting) cream suit, stocking-clad legs — even I had had more sense than to contemplate tights for such a journey — to my strapped, open-toed cream shoes.

'Yes, well,' he said. He spoke slowly, I had already noticed, so that his voice carried with it a leisurely, almost casual ease of manner that was oddly soothing. One felt involuntarily that there was really nothing at all to worry about, and all the time in the world to do it in, even if there were.

When he smiled at me it was as he had smiled at Dora's kitten in its basket (and as the adjective kittenish was the one I would have imagined to be the least likely to be applied to me by any of my acquaintance I found it a disconcertingly new experience). I smiled back in the slightly frosty manner that shyness invariably produces in me as he switched the cat basket to his left hand and held out his right.

'Nicholas Locke,' he said. 'And you'll be Miss Callow, I'm thinking?'

I nodded faintly, trying to hide my incredulity. There was, when one thought about it, no valid reason why I should have supposed the man mentioned in Lowell and Driscoll's letter to be a contemporary of my father's, but there it was. I had pictured a shabby, leathery-skinned backwoods type in faded jeans, with stubble on his chin and an inarticulate tongue, and the revelation that he was a bare five or six years older than myself took getting used to.

'How d'you do?'

He nodded. 'Hi. This is Dora Bannister. Lives on a farm outside town.' He shook his head at me. 'You didn't actually have to *come*, you know. All you needed to do was write. Jerry Driscoll's a pal of mine; he'd have kept me posted.'

'You don't seem all that surprised to see me, just the same. You knew who I was.'

'Not very difficult. Jerry told me about your cable when I got in from the valley, and' — his wide mouth twitched with amusement — 'Minzanda gets a bit short on tourists, come late

October. Visitors are few and far between.'

Dora and the Customs man chuckled appreciatively at this sally, while I looked at them a little uncertainly. There were, by now, only the four of us left, and now Dora, clicking her tongue, scooped her hand luggage together and scuttled towards the doors.

'I'll be late.' She turned to regard me with her kind brown eyes. 'If you're here any time at all I'll be seeing you again, love. So long.'

The Customs man lifted the flap of his counter, stepped through to our side, and lowered it with a slam of finality.

'That's all for today, then.' He nodded at Nicholas Locke, beamed at me, picked up his cap and strode away.

'Now,' said my companion, 'let's get you into town. I'm afraid it's a Land-Rover, and a bit dusty at that.' He eyed my suit doubtfully. 'Will that wash?'

I laughed. I was obviously going to be

obliged to abandon my elegant London image while in Minzanda, and it might as well be sooner or later.

'I've never tried. But the label says it will.'

His brow cleared. 'That's all right, then. I've got some sacks in the back, but they'll probably be even dustier than the seat.'

He shook his head at a white-clad porter as he approached, picked up my case in his free hand and loped away on his incredibly long legs towards the entrance and out on to the wide asphalt walk. I followed meekly, feeling the heat like a blast from a gigantic oven as I stepped outside after him.

Very little of the original grey of the Land-Rover was visible under the blanket of reddish-brown grime. It was the dirtiest vehicle I had ever seen, and I wondered what conceivable climatic conditions could possibly have produced such an effect under less than a period of months. Then I remembered the clouds of dust that enveloped the cars I had glimpsed from the Dakota, and was not quite so incredulous.

He threw open the passenger seat door and leaned inside to put cat basket and case in the back beside a pile of heterogeneous gear such as I could not even begin to identify. Then he turned and remarked cheerfully:

'Ever climbed into a Land-Rover?' I shook my head.

'Well, you won't make it in that skirt unless you hitch it a bit.'

He was right. Pink with annoyance and embarrassment, I tried to reach the step with one hand lifting the hem of my skirt a couple of inches. Even with *my* legs it was impossible. Finally, while he stood patiently holding the door, I gripped the wretched garment with both hands, hitched it up to my thighs, and lunged upwards with one foot. At exactly the right moment he put a hand under my elbow and lifted me on to the step. The impetus shot me into the vehicle and on to the seat in one ungraceful, upward dive.

'Well done.' He slammed the door, walked round and climbed into the driver's seat, and inched the Land-Rover past a miscellany of crates and trollies and out on to the dirt road beyond.

If one ignored the dust — and that at least we left bellying out behind us — the road was fairly good. Apart from one widish turn-off which led to a cluster of surprisingly pleasant-looking single-storey houses there seemed to be nothing but the road itself, sloping steadily downhill all the way, and the dust-laden bush that stretched on either side.

He gestured towards the turn-off as we passed it. 'Airport staff houses,' he explained, after which conversation languished until the first traces of Chundi came into view.

These began with a scattering of houses set in large and surprisingly attractive gardens on either side of the road, followed by a glimpse of metalled roadway ahead. For the final half-mile the descent was a steep one, and I remarked that Chundi appeared to lie in a valley.

'Well. A basin, sort of. That's why it's so hot at this time of year. Much cooler at the airport.'

Remembering the temperature outside the airport buildings, I found this remark somewhat less than reassuring, and contented myself with looking about me as we turned into the main street.

It was an attractive place, I found, somewhat to my surprise. Stucco shop and office fronts jostled each other behind wide, high-kerbed pavements that were shaded, for the most part, by the addition of arcades supported on pillars set in the kerb.

People, mostly women and children, moved in and out of the shops, their gay cotton dresses bright against the colour-washed buildings. To my eyes, however, the most attractive thing about the street was the line of trees that graced the centre of the wide roadway as far as the eye could reach.

They were set close enough so that the wide, spreading branches interlocked, making a cool green tunnel of shade under which cars were parked, forming a dual carriageway, and sprays of brilliant flame-red blossom cascaded along the branches, weighing them down in places. A scattering of fallen blossom lay on the glittering metal of the roadway.

'They're beautiful,' I said, entranced. 'That's flame lily colour, isn't it?'

'M'mm? Oh, the flamboyants. Yes. Means the rains will start any time now. The blossom doesn't last long after that.'

He was slowing now, taking a dip in the roadway carefully as we approached a turning on the left.

'What *are* those dips? They go right across the street, don't they?'

'Yes. Gets the water away quicker. Into the storm drains along the kerbs. See 'em?' He took the turning, drove along for a hundred or so yards, and came to a halt where the road widened into a kind of forecourt before a long, low building.

'Blake's,' he said, flicking the door wide and beginning to climb down.

'Will they have room?'

'Nothing but.' He laughed as he walked round to help me down. 'I told you. Minzanda hasn't much except tourism, and it's a bit late in the year for that, with the rains on us any time now.'

He flapped a hand behind him at the Land-Rover as we walked toward's Blake's. 'Had a shower or two in the valley before I got away. Hence the mud.'

It was the second time he had mentioned the valley. I wanted desperately to ask him about it; about my father and if that was where he had met him, but some instinct warned me against questioning him yet. Besides, I told myself, I ought really to call upon Lowell and Driscoll, the solicitors who had made contact with me in the first place, before asking any questions.

But in my heart I knew well enough what my real motive was in waiting. I wanted my father to be alive, and until I actually asked if he were, I could go on pretending. Once they told me he was dead (and, like my mother, reason told me that he must be), all pretence would be over; I would have to accept it.

And yet, as I stood beside Nicholas Locke at the reception desk in the dim, and surprisingly cool, foyer, I found myself wondering what, if he were indeed dead, had caused Mr Jerome Driscoll to use the word urgent in his letter to me.

This, at least, I could ask. Or could I? Might the answer not give me the very information I did not want to hear? Yet, if he was dead, how could anything be urgent? There is nothing less urgent than the state of death.

My hopes began to rise again. I turned to ask my first question relating to my reason for being there just as the Minzandan clerk behind the desk pushed the register towards me. 'Sign, please, Madam.'

'Right.' Nicholas Locke, having personally seen me disposed of to his satisfaction, gave my shoulder a farewell pat. 'I'll be off home, then. Haven't been there yet since I got in.'

'Mr Locke. Wait. Why did you — ?'

'Sorry. No more time. Need a bath, too. Haven't had one for a week.' My jaw must have dropped; he grinned and added: 'Fact. Not my fault. Ran out of water.'

'Ran out?' I believed he was joking.

'Well, let's say the river did.'

'You mean it dried up? Completely?'

'That's right. They do, you know. All the time, in the dry season.'

'But — all at once? Just like that?'

'We-ell. Not exactly. One finds a puddle or two here and there.' He looked amused. 'Then the puddles disappear and one digs.'

'Digs?' I was repeating myself like a halfwit.

'Digs. Haven't you ever dug in the

sand at the seaside as a child when the tide's gone out, and found water?'

'Oh, I see.'

'Doubt if you do, really. The sea comes back before the sand dries out very deeply. A dried-up river bed in Africa; that's something else again. It simply gets drier and drier.'

'But what did you use for drinking?'

'Yes, well. That does get a little awkward from time to time, I must say. Depends whereabouts in the corridor one happens to be, of course. This time — '

'What corridor?' I stopped myself, just in time, from simply repeating 'corridor?' like the parrot I seemed to have become.

'Tsetse corridor. We move about, you see. Naturally.'

'Naturally,' I repeated, dazed.

'So sometimes we're fairly near a camp.' He paused, then added: 'a game reserve camp, where there's a borehole.'

'Oh.'

'But this time the nearest drinking

water was over thirty miles away, and over the most terrible road — track — I've ever battled along. So you see, we had to be content with filling our water bags and containers, and using it very cannily indeed.'

'But wouldn't *they* have let you take a bath?'

'Who?'

'The people.'

'Which — ? Oh, you mean where we found the water? Just an old disused tin mine, I'm afraid. No — er — bath.' The silver-grey eyes held a disconcerting twinkle; I realised, to my discomfort, that I was still not sure whether I was having my leg pulled or not. Whatever the case I was completely out of my depth, as I suspected he well knew, and judged it high time to change the subject.

'Of *course* I mustn't keep you. You've been — most kind. I'm sorry I've delayed you. But — '

'Not at all. Pleasure.' He turned away again.

'It's just — when can we talk about my father?'

'Ah. Sorry. I meant to tell you. That's why I popped into Jerry's office — to see if he'd heard from you. Then he told me you'd cabled you were coming out and might even be on today's plane. So we arranged to come over here together this evening after dinner; eight-thirty suit you?'

'Yes. Mr Locke, wait. Is my father alive?'

He paused in his stride, glanced at me over his shoulder, said: 'Well, that's what we still have to find out, I'm afraid. But he was, a few weeks ago;' and went.

Slightly taken aback by this businesslike display of hustle from a man who had struck me up to now as being casual in the extreme, I followed the waiting porter towards my room.

Blake's annexe proved to be a group of a dozen or so whitewashed, thatched, round huts — my mother's rondavels, I thought, with a sense of half-recognition — scattered about a rectangular yard or compound behind the hotel proper.

The interior was attractive and surprisingly roomy. The stone-like floor was a highly polished red, and a mosquito net was suspended above the well-sprung bed, the material looped into a loose knot below its frame. The two windows set into the curved walls were gauzed, and a door between led into the smallest — and most oddly-shaped — bathroom I had ever seen. Two or three wide rugs were scattered about, and the bedside switch worked when I tried it. The place was scrupulously — almost clinically — clean.

But there was no ceiling. I stared apprehensively up into the cone-shaped mat of dark thatch above my head and wondered what particular species of beetle-like horrors it might be harbouring. I had always been a coward about crawlies. Best not to think about it, I decided, and, lowering my eyes resolutely, I began to unpack while my thoughts dwelt upon the coming meeting with Mr Locke and Mr Driscoll, and whatever significant information they may have for me regarding my father.

5

Piano music drifted down upon us from an antiquated recording system as we sat beneath the ceiling fans in the hotel lounge, as near to one of the five wide-open french doors as it was possible for us to get. I was just able to discern the strains of 'Too Many Rings Around Rosie' against the chirping of crickets and a high, incessant shrilling sound that Jerome Driscoll and Nicholas Locke — 'Jerry and Nick, please' — assured me came from the cicadas hidden among the branches of the gnarled indigenous trees dotted about the yard outside.

'Do they make that noise all the time?'

'Off and on, around this time of year.' Jerry Driscoll grinned at me. He was an exceptionally good-looking man — probably a little older than Nicholas

Locke — whom I had found myself liking on sight. Sun-bleached fair hair against a brown tan was always effective, I thought as I smiled back at him.

'I shall never sleep through that.'

'Oh, you will, once you get used to 'em. Thing is, they have a trick of stopping all at once just as you've dropped off, and that wakes you, so you have to start all over again.'

I was beginning to grow accustomed to the slightly bantering, good-humoured manner that seemed prevalent among such Europeans as I had met so far. The Minzandans appeared to match it with a wit of their own; there had been quite a bout of repartee in the vernacular, of which I had not understood a word, between Nick and Jerry and the waiter who brought our coffee and liqueurs soon after they arrived.

But they could be serious, too, and were, while they told me the little there was to tell about their reasons for tracing me in England.

'They pop in and out all the time, these prospectors, in the corridor, you understand. They need someone to talk to occasionally, I suppose,' said Nick.

He had already explained the tsetse corridor as a thirty-mile-wide strip lying between the game reserve (which happened to be Loni Game Park, one of the wildest and most famous in Africa, and of which even I had heard) and the cattle ranch grazing areas beyond. Tsetse fly being a deadly enemy to cattle, said Nick, the corridor was for their protection against it. I was interested enough to want to ask more, but far too anxious about what they could tell me about my father to pursue it for the moment.

'And *this* man popped up?'

'Well. In a way. But he wasn't looking for company, I'd say, so much as someone to whom he could give a message.

'He asked one of our hunters if the veterinary surgeon was available — knowing, I suppose, that I'd probably be leaving for town sooner than any of the others; they get to know the routine out there — and he sent him over to me.'

'What did he look like?' Not that it would help much; I had never seen a photograph of my father. If my mother had ever possessed any, and she had not admitted to this, they had been destroyed many years ago, she said. To my astonished: 'Not even a wedding photograph?' she had replied tersely that there had been a war on.

I had enough sense to know that, as an excuse, this was puerile, but had to let it pass.

'I couldn't see him properly. Never saw a man so covered in hair. Couldn't have shaved for years. He was just acting as a messenger, anyway. He handed me this blank cheque — must have been from about the oldest cheque book in circulation. Yellow with age, for one thing, and for another they just don't make 'em like that any more.

'Anyway, it was signed A. G. Callow,

and drawn on the Chundi Branch of Emerson's Bank. He said there would be ample funds to meet it and that this chap he'd got it from wanted you traced.'

'But who *was* he? The man who gave it to you? Did you ask?'

'Said his name was Kelly. Prospecting for tin. There are quite a few disused tin mines in the area, and one still in operation up near the hundred-mile peg.'

'What's a peg?'

Jerry leaned forward to interrupt. 'There are some pretty wild outposts in Africa. Not a town, not even a settlement or village. There isn't a lot of sense in giving names to wide-open spaces, or miles of bush where nobody lives.

'But of course there has to be some sort of identification for people working in the field. And the farmers name their ranches; that helps. A farmer called — say — Johnson loads his maize or cotton or tobacco on to trucks at a railway siding on his land that's there especially for him, and it becomes Johnson's Siding, or possibly the name he's given his ranch. It all helps to identify an area. The hundred-mile peg is simply a spot one hundred miles out from Chundi. In other words, it's in the middle of nowhere.'

'I see.' Indeed, I felt that I was really only just beginning to. 'This man Kelly. Didn't you know him? Had you never seen him before?'

'Not that I know of. It was dark, too, you know. There was only the light from our camp fires so that I couldn't see much; and he wouldn't let me get too close. Tall, but stooped, and I fancied he was a little drunk.' He paused, as if unsure about this.

'Drunk? Oh.' My heart sank. A drunkard's tale —

'Not very. Nothing out of the way in fact, for that time of the evening in that part of the world.' Nick smiled; a compassionate sort of smile. 'What else is there for them to do when the sun goes down and the mosquitoes start to nibble, or they feel a touch of malaria coming on? He knew what he was saying, all right, and he said it was very urgent. Very urgent indeed.'

'Did you ask him why?'

'I did indeed. I asked him if the fellow was ill, or dying, or something. For one thing, I couldn't see why he couldn't have come himself. Well, he said he *might* be.'

'What do you suppose he meant?' I studied their faces anxiously.

Jerry cleared his throat. 'Could be any one of a number of things.' He hesitated, then plunged on. 'Look, this is Africa. There's a Mission just above the valley, run by White Fathers, nuns and brothers, and a couple of lay doctors for the Leprosarium nearby.'

He saw the shudder I could not repress, and stopped. Then I caught Nick's eye. He was shaking his head at me reprovingly.

'You know,' he said, 'you really ought to have grown out of it by now. Never

97

let the mere *name* of a disease frighten or shock you. Besides — '

'I know. I'm sorry. It's just — '

'Besides,' he went on as though I had not spoken, 'leprosy is curable these days if it's caught in time, just like T.B. Also like T.B., it isn't nearly as contagious as people used to believe. That there are still lepers in Africa at all is a damn' sad thing, because in the developed areas it is being stamped out entirely.

'But out in the sticks — well, that's another matter. Some of the poor devils are too ignorant to know anything's wrong until it's too late. Then they think they're bewitched, maybe, and consult their witchdoctors — ' He shook his head again, then smiled reassuringly.

'Anyway, if your father leads as solitary a life as a lot of these chaps out there, there's absolutely no reason to think it's anything like that at all. Perhaps he's weak from — oh — recurrent bouts of malaria or something. Or it might be just that he feels he's getting on a bit. How old would he be? D'you know?' Nick looked at me from under his deep brows, and waited.

They had trodden very carefully so far regarding my side of the matter. Indeed, this was the first even remotely personal question that had been asked of me. That had not prevented me from sensing a reserve at my obvious lack of knowledge regarding my own father. It must have seemed to these young men, with their warm, human attitude of involvement with anyone in trouble or in need, unnatural in the extreme.

'My mother divorced my father when I was a little girl,' I said carefully. 'She married again. He was — is — older than she is. About fifty-nine or sixty, perhaps.'

'I see.' Nick moved his elbows from the table as the waiter came to take away our coffee cups and glasses, watching the man's deft movements thoughtfully. 'Not a great age, then.'

'This man — the bearded man — did

he come back?' I asked, aware that my reluctance to say more about my lifelong ignorance regarding my father — or the reasons for it at this stage — had not passed unnoticed.

'No. No, he didn't. At least he hasn't so far. Perhaps he's giving us time. To trace you.'

'But if it's so urgent you'd have thought — '

'Yes. That *had* occurred to me, too. But I'm not out there all the time, you see. I come into Chundi every three weeks or so for a few days. There are blood samples or pathological material to be brought in — '

'What is it that you do, then, in the valley? Test the wild life for tsetse — er — ?'

'Tryps? Trypanosoma? That's the tsetse parasite.'

'Oh. Yes. Isn't that sleeping sickness? Or what causes it?'

'Broadly speaking. Only certain types of tryps affect human beings, though. But our concern is with animals — I'm a vet, remember.' He put his elbows back on the table and leaned forward. At the same moment Jerry caught my eye and winked solemnly, as though Nick were about to mount his hobby horse.

'The corridor is there solely for the protection of cattle against the disease; Nagana, as it's called, in animals. The parasite is carried by host animals who act as carriers. Cattle are very vulnerable indeed to the tsetse parasite.'

'And the wild animals pass it on to cattle, you mean?'

'Yes. Not all wild life; giraffe, for example, do not carry the parasite. So not all game reserves have tsetse.'

'So how do you know which *are* carrying it?'

'We know which are likely to. Bush buck, kudu and wild pig for instance. And wart hog, elephant, buffalo — '

'And you try to cure them in the corridor?'

'No, no. As I said, they are not diseased in themselves. Besides — ' His eyes held a gleam of amusement, while Jerry began to laugh.

'Try curing an African elephant of anything, anyway,' he said, 'and see where it gets you. Or buffalo for that matter. You'll end up needing a cure yourself.'

I joined in their laughter. 'So you keep this corridor for — ?'

'We keep the corridor clear.'

'Oh. You drive the wild life back into the reserve?'

'No. We shoot them. That's what the hunters — field officers — are for.'

'Shoot them? Kill them, you mean? What, all of them?' I stared at him unbelievingly.

'All of them. All host game are listed as carriers, but while they remain in Loni reserve all is well. Beyond this point a thirty-mile corridor has been declared, which runs along the entire length of the reserve. We have a heavy steel fence erected that prevents game from moving beyond this point. On the other side of the fence cattle may graze, but even then only under constant supervision. The field officers patrol that area, too, and what is called controlled hunting is carried out there.' He paused, in his slow, deliberate fashion, as though to let this sink in, then added:

'But *inside* the fence — in the corridor — all host animals are killed out. It's the only way.' He must have seen the expression on my face.

'Do — do *you* shoot them?'

From the way his mouth twisted it struck me that I had touched a raw spot.

'Sometimes. When I have to.'

'But I thought game preservation meant keeping them alive.' I could hear the indignation in my voice as I spoke, and broke off, confused.

'And so it does, but it's a great deal more complicated than that. When conditions are perfect, or nearly, as in a game park like Loni, you can end up with more than the reserve can carry.' He grinned at me cheeringly. 'You know, it's a bit like this population explosion we all keep hearing about.' The smile vanished as he added: 'Except that we haven't started killing off surplus humanity yet. Or only under licence, as it were.'

'You don't like it.'

'The killing part? No. But I *can* see that it has to be done.'

'Do you go out to the valley all through the year?'

'Not once the rains begin. Unless there's an emergency. An outbreak of nagana beyond the fence for example. It has been known.'

'But the field officers — they stay?'

'Yes. All the time, to keep the corridor clear, otherwise we'd be overrun again by the time the dry season came round.'

I sank back into my chair, trying to digest what I had been told, and wondering if it had been like this in my mother's day. The two men waited, in their unhurried, leisurely way, for my next question. After the rush and bustle of my London office and the irascibility of Mr Mostyn, they seemed to me to be the most patient men I had ever met.

'So if this man came back — Kelly, wasn't it? — while you were here in town, he'd find somebody there?'

'Oh, yes. Sure to, if he looked about a bit. But it's a pretty nomad sort of existence in the valley, you see. They live under mobile conditions, moving from one place to another as animals are sighted. And I have to move with them when I'm there. I *must* be on hand as they are shot to take blood or pathological samples, and so on.'

'What for?'

'Researching the incidence of infection in game animals is the whole object of the operation, as far as Nick's concerned,' Jerry told me.

'And when do you go back again?'

'Probably about Wednesday. If the rains don't beat me to it.' He leaned back and beckoned a nearby waiter.

'All this talking's made me dry.' His eyes crinkled at me. 'I'm not used to it after three weeks in the bush. What'll you have? It's lager for Jerry and me; I know that. Oh, come on,' as I hesitated while the waiter hovered. 'You must have a nightcap.'

'It'll help you to sleep,' said Jerry, jerking his head in the direction of the still-shrilling cicadas. 'You'll need it.'

And as a matter of fact I did, though not entirely because of the cicadas. I had, in fact, already begun to grow accustomed to the sound. It was the thatch above my bed that worried me. From time to time there came a sinister rustling sound which startled me into wakefulness just as I was growing drowsy. A mouse? Or worse, a rat? Worst of all, could it be a bat? Or bats?

Each time I closed my eyes it was to picture a horde of the horrid creatures flitting back and forth inside the cone of blackness above my head. Each time I put out my hand to switch on the light I drew it tremblingly back again, realising that on the whole I would rather not know if it were so. In the end, of course, I fell asleep from sheer exhaustion; and, mice, rats, bats and cicadas notwithstanding, slept like a log until morning.

* * *

A white-clad waiter delivered a tray of tea to my rondavel at the unearthly hour of six-thirty, and informed me that breakfast was served between seven o'clock and eight-thirty.

I had for some time been aware of a clumping sound from the direction of the bathroom. I entered and peered through the open window to see a contraption of bricks upon which rested what appeared to be an oil drum lying on its side. A wood fire blazed in the space between the drum and the brick support, and a weird arrangement of pipes travelled from the drum and out of sight beneath my window.

The ease with which I recognised it as my hot-water system surprised me.

Had I seen one before, all those years ago? I turned on the hot tap, searching my memory in vain. One thing was certain, however; it worked. The water was piping hot, and there was far more of it than I needed.

As I bathed and dressed I worked out my plan of campaign. I was to call in at the offices of Lowell and Driscoll at ten: but first I would do some shopping.

The contents of my case were grossly unsuitable for the heat; already the sun was up and the glare from its rays upon the white-painted rondavels around me was considerable. Even the thinnest of my slacks would be too hot; bare legs were obviously the thing. Bare legs and no sleeves; all my dresses had sleeves.

So I must shop for sandals and two or three sleeveless cotton dresses. That was the first thing.

The next was to persuade Nicholas Locke to take me out to the valley with him on Wednesday.

I had not dared to broach the matter

the night before. I had caught both men's eyes upon me more than once, appraising me in the manner of men with a girl anywhere in the world, and what I had seen in their glances had not been altogether reassuring.

There had been approval, certainly, of my thin green silk dress, but their eyes had lingered upon silvered nails and silver evening shoes, and upon my pale, piled-up hair almost with awe. Since I could never be petite and cuddly like my mother, and so many of the pretty girls I knew, I had long ago settled for the only possible thing for a girl nearly six feet tall, and made elegance my watchword, so that it had now become a habit.

Somehow, therefore, I did not see a trip into the wilds of the African bush as being in accord with the picture that had already been formed in their minds — especially Nick's — of an impeccably groomed, London-orientated female. So I should have to do something to change it, or I had not a hope of persuading him to let me accompany him.

* * *

Jerry Driscoll was apparently the type to revert to formality behind his office desk. Indeed, with hornrimmed spectacles bridging his nose and a veritable wall of law books behind him, he did not at first seem to be the same man.

'Please sit down, Miss Callow. Would you like coffee?'

I shook my head, annoyed with myself for allowing such a familiarly-businesslike setting to dampen my spirits. After all these years I should be used enough to it, heaven knew. Nevertheless, as I sat down in the chair opposite his I found myself almost groping for my notebook and pencil. Mr Mostyn had never been a dictaphone enthusiast.

But I *had* given myself a new image, and I felt that Mr Jerome Driscoll should have recognised the fact. Surely, with bare toes wriggling beneath a mere suggestion of white strapping, and in a sleeveless white cotton dress splashed with sunflowers nearly as large as life, and with my hair brushed casually away from my face, I looked more the kind of young woman who might be expected to want to view Africa in the wild?

Apparently not. 'Mr Driscoll,' I began firmly. To my relief he looked up from the file on his desk, stared at me through the owl-like spectacles, and said reproachfully: 'I thought we'd agreed on Jerry.'

'Well. So did I. In that case, I'm Emma.'

'Emma. Emma Jane. You know, I like that.'

'You do?'

'Very much. Look — er — Emma, I want to ask you a few questions regarding your father. I am assuming you're anxious to get in touch with him as soon as possible?'

'Of course. That's why I'm here. But I can't tell you much. You see — '

'Did your mother live here in Minzanda with him at any time?'

'Yes. So did I, for that matter.'

He was clearly surprised. 'I hadn't realised that. You've been in Africa before then? And it never occurred to me. Nor Nick, I'm pretty sure.'

I shook my head. 'I was only four when — when my mother took me back to England. I don't really remember my father at all, let alone Africa.'

'No, I see. What did he do?'

'He was a field officer.'

'Was he, indeed?' This appeared to interest him.

'Yes, but he got what my mother called the prospecting bug — '

Jerry laughed. 'Ah, yes. Quarter of a century or so ago there'd be a lot of them about.'

'Aren't there still?'

'We-ell. Yes and no. Plenty of serious, down-to-earth prospectors. But the gold-and-diamond-rush syndrome petered out quite a while back. What was he prospecting for — tin?'

112

'No. Diamonds.'

I recognised the look on his face the second it appeared. One of *those*, it seemed to say. His opinion of my father would, I felt sure, follow the same course as my mother's from now on.

'But there *are* diamonds in Africa,' I said defensively.

'In some parts of Africa, true.' He hesitated. 'Don't get me wrong. I'm not saying that in his time there may not have been some sort of grounds for belief that diamonds might be found around here. For that matter a South African firm has been prospecting in this country for many years.'

'And they found nothing?'

'I wouldn't say that.' He picked up the telephone. 'Bring some tea, please.' He smiled at me. 'You'll drink tea with me now, won't you?'

I nodded, smiling back at him. 'So what *did* they find?'

'Oh, plenty of diamonds of the industrial kind. Very small stuff indeed. They're still finding 'em I believe. But no gemstones, as far as I know.'

Something stirred in my mind. 'If my father was prospecting somewhere on his own he'd need a licence, wouldn't he?'

'Indeed he would.' He looked at me rather searchingly.

'And nobody else could prospect there?'

'Quite right. He would be granted — let's see. The law's changed very little in Minzanda since then. In all the independent states, of course, it's quite different now.' He reached behind him and pulled out a book from one of the shelves, flicking the pages and muttering to himself in that knowledgeable way solicitors always seem to possess.

'Yes. A deed of special grant. There'd be a sketch plan of the area, together with a description of its extent, location, and so on.'

'Could he — would he actually own any diamonds he found?'

'Oh, yes. There'd be a royalty, of course, and he'd be obliged to declare all findings monthly.' He gave me another long, considering look, his eyes cool and assessing behind the spectacles.

'But they'd be his? To sell, or — '

'They'd be his.' There was a tap on the door, and a Minzandan in a khaki uniform emblazoned with 'Messenger' on the pocket in red, entered with a tray.

'Wouldn't he need a mining licence as well?'

He shook his head. 'Milk?' I took my cup from him and sipped the tea, concentrating fiercely. Somewhere there must be a record —

'The grant would cover mining, too. 'Sole and exclusive rights to prospect and mine for, work, extract, keep and dispose of diamonds in, under or upon diamondiferous ground — ' That's the way it goes, more or less.'

Another thought struck me. 'For how long? I mean, is it like a TV licence, for instance?'

Jerry frowned and put down his cup.

'Now you've got me. I'm not at all sure how long. I'm reasonably certain that in the old days the big boys — the large, moneyed companies from South Africa for instance — would have had them granted in perpetuity. But lone prospectors — ' He shook his head. 'Five years, perhaps. Maybe ten. I could find out.'

I was becoming too excited, suddenly, to smile at all the legal jargon. 'Say five years. Then he'd have to renew, wouldn't he? Five fives are twenty-five — say he took out his first licence a year before my mother took me back to England. That would mean he'd have had to renew as recently as a year ago.'

I pushed my cup aside and shook my head as he indicated the teapot.

'Where could I find out? Where are the records kept?'

'At the Registry of Mining Titles. But wait a bit, you're going too fast.'

'Why am I? He would have to, wouldn't he?'

'He *wouldn't* have to, now would he? Only if he wanted to continue prospecting.'

'But — but that's the whole — '

'Twenty-five years is a long time for one man to continue prospecting over the same area of ground, however badly the bug had bitten him. Especially if he'd found nothing.'

'But he may have been finding diamonds during that time for all we know.'

Jerry emptied his cup and set it down carefully. 'And nobody's ever heard of the rich diamond strike in Minzanda?' He regarded me sadly, then, as though seeing the eagerness die out of my face, added on a more cheerful note:

'But it's worth following up. At least we can find out when he last took out a licence. Leave it to me, will you? I'll make a search and let you know.'

As he saw me out into the blazing street he rested a hand briefly on my shoulder.

'It may turn out a lot easier than we think. It's entirely possible that by the time Nick gets out to the valley on

Wednesday Kelly will have popped up again.' He gave me another searching look, smiled a brief goodbye and disappeared inside the building.

If he's stayed sober long enough, I found myself thinking a little bitterly as I turned away; if he's an alcoholic he may *never* come back.

I walked slowly back to Blake's, hugging the shade as far as I was able. Even so, by the time I entered the hotel my dress was clinging uncomfortably to my body and the hair at the back of my neck felt sodden.

All at once the fact that there was nothing more that I could do until I saw Nick to talk him into taking me out to the valley, that tomorrow was Sunday and it was highly unlikely Jerry would have any information for me regarding the licence before Monday, ceased to matter quite so acutely. I was hot, tired and thirsty. I ordered a long, chilled lemonade, wandered away to my rondavel, pulled off my sandals and dress, and lay down on the bed.

6

A little to my surprise — and disappointment — I saw neither of them during the weekend. Realising that it had been foolish of me to expect to (they belonged in Chundi, and would have their own circle of friends and family. Indeed, for all I knew, they may both be married men with wives and children to occupy their whole attention); I found the church and attended ten o'clock service.

To my delight Dora — Mrs Bannister — was there with her husband. She greeted me like a long-lost friend in the porch afterwards, introduced me to her Frank, a weather-beaten man of fifty or so, took me by the hand to meet the priest, and insisted that I travel out to their farm for Sunday midday dinner. They would bring me back safely, they assured me, before dark.

And so, instead of the lonely, aimless Sunday I had been expecting, I spent a pleasant day lolling around the Bannister's large, shady veranda and eating far more than I would have dreamed myself capable of tucking away in such heat. I travelled down with Frank during the afternoon in the hay-laden truck and watched the Minzandan farm workers toss the bales into the corral for the dairy cattle, while Dora, I suspect, enjoyed a short nap.

'No grazing for them now till the rains begin,' he said.

'When will that be, d'you think?'

'Oh, soon. It builds up for several days, and the heat begins to get sticky and humid.'

'I thought it already had,' I remarked dryly. He took my words seriously.

'Yes, well. It's beginning to.' He cast a look at the brassy, cloudless sky. 'Soon, I'm thinking. About a week, perhaps; not much longer than that.'

In view of my determination to accompany Nick to the valley, this was not precisely what I wished to hear, and I pondered it while Frank drove me back to Blake's that evening with Dora sitting beside me, chattering about Minzanda, the farm, and Chundi.

I had already learned that both Jerry and Nick were unattached. Jerry, she told me, had been engaged to Charles Lowell's granddaughter — 'Charles has been dead these ten years or more — 'but she had gone away to University in Natal, met somebody else, and that was that. He now looked, in her opinion, all set for bachelorhood.

'The truth is,' she informed me, 'that there simply aren't enough girls to go round in a place like this. Three to one, I believe the ratio is. Is that right, Frank?'

Her husband grunted. 'Trouble is, the girls don't care to settle here. Off they go to study in South Africa, or England, and after about a year away what attractions can a country like Minzanda have? Can't blame 'em really.'

'But surely that applies even more to young men?'

'We-ell. Only up to a point. You see, this is an agricultural country in the main. There's very little mineral wealth — or if there is it's still to be found. A little tin here and there, and of course there's Loni, which really is bringing in the type of back-to-nature tourist who likes his wild life a little wilder than in the big reserves further south, where I believe things are beginning to get so commercialised that the game all but come up to you and eat out of your hand.'

'So — ?'

'In other words,' put in Dora, 'this is a man's country still, and there's getting to be precious few of those left. The farmer's sons come back to farm, used to the outdoor life and wide open spaces, and the young men come out from Britain looking for a more exciting and roomy existence — like Nick Locke for example — to see a bit of the world and widen their experience. That sort of adventure's not so easy to find if you're a girl, even in these days.'

'How long has he been here?' Suddenly I remembered the Scottish accent; he had seemed to me so much a part of his surroundings that, apart from it, he might almost have been born in Africa, he had seemed to me to be so much at home here.

'This'll be his second tour.' Frank changed down to take the hump from dirt to tarmac as we reached the almost deserted Chundi road. 'Three-year stretch, that is.'

'But he'll go back to Britain on leave and get married to some little provincial lass and settle down there in the end, you mark my words,' said Dora. 'The ones from Britain nearly always do, even when they like the life out here as much as he does.'

'Perhaps he'll come back with a bride,' I suggested lightly as Frank pulled up in Blake's forecourt.

He turned and grinned at me as though I had made a witty remark.

'He'll be lucky. They won't come, you know. What, leave swinging Britain for this? Would you?'

Without waiting for a reply he slid out from behind the wheel and was opening my door before I had time to locate the handle. I thought fleetingly of my mother and looked back at Dora questioningly.

'If she cared about him enough — ' I stopped as she leaned forward and, to my surprise and pleasure, kissed me warmly on the cheek.

'Ah, in that case — Who's to say? But we have our faults too, don't we? We're apt to marry a man and then start trying to make him live the kind of life *we'd* like. Suburban semi-detached with the school and supermarket not too far away, and a nice white-collar job for him with good prospects and regular hours. The poor suckers don't stand a chance with us, do they?'

Frank was laughing over my shoulder at her as he slid a hand beneath my elbow to assist me out of the car.

'Not Dora, though. I picked her up in Middlesbrough when I was over in Britain twelve years ago, and she's stuck it ever since.' He winked at me. 'Mind you, I take good care she never gets a chance to raise the fare home.'

Dora gave him a withering glance. 'What d'you mean, home? I *am* home.' She grinned at me. 'And with Frank's brother and his wife to visit in Salisbury, what more do I want?'

Children? I wondered, remembering the kitten as I thanked them both and waved them out of sight. They were plainly a devoted couple, yet there had been no trace — or mention — of offspring at the farm. I sat around for a while in the lounge, lingering over my after-dinner coffee in the faint hope that Nick or Jerry, or both, might put in an appearance. In the end sheer sleepiness drove me to my rondavel where, in spite of the heat, I fell asleep even before it occurred to me to strain my ears for sinister rustling sounds from the thatch above my head.

* ★ ★ ★

Jerry Driscoll rang me just as I had finished breakfast the following morning. Business hours, it appeared, began a great deal earlier in Chundi than in London. Prospector's licences, he informed me, were granted for a ten-year period. My father had taken out two; one in 1947 and the second ten years later. The copy sketch plan included an area known locally as Diamond Hill, though it was in fact no more than a longish, flat-topped hillock of the kind, said Jerry, that were often to be seen popping up amidst the plains and valleys of Africa.

'So he no longer has a licence for that area?' Now why was that, I wondered? Jerry cut in on my thoughts.

'He no longer has one at all. There's a twenty-acre plot adjoining Diamond Hill. I checked on the farm number in the Deeds Registry. The freehold is vested in the name of Andrew Grant Callow.'

'Er — you mean he owns it?'

'That's right.'

'So he's farming? But surely twenty acres wouldn't be — '

'Sorry again. Plots of that size — outside a municipal boundary — are designated farms or smallholdings. It doesn't mean he's farming, I assure you. Oh, and something else.' He had come upon one of the hunters, he said, who was spending a weekend in Chundi and leaving again for the valley this very morning.

'Nick has them all pretty well clued-up about this chap Kelly, but I thought it would do no harm to tell him that you've arrived out here trying to locate your father, and to try and hang on to Kelly if he turns up. If not, to ask him for Mr Callow's whereabouts. Greg Tarrant — this hunter — says he'll do his best.'

I thanked him. 'Has he left yet? This Mr Tarrant? I'd have liked to talk to him.'

There was a faint cough from the

127

other end of the line. 'Oh, yes. He'd leave about dawn, before it gets too hot. Come to think of it, he'd heard you'd arrived. A female arrival in these parts causes great excitement, you know.'

'And I was here at Blake's from six onwards yesterday. What a pity I didn't know.'

'M'mm? Oh, well.' There was the slightest of pauses. 'Some of these fellows are a bit on the rough and ready side, you know. I thought perhaps he — er — wouldn't be quite your type.'

I felt a spurt of annoyance which I tried to stifle before asking lightly: 'And what type is that, Jerry?'

There was another pause before he added, with a light laugh: 'Oh, well. Fresh from London and all cover-girl and glossy.'

I stood silently for a moment, reflecting that the Jerry Driscoll of this morning was not, in some indefinable way, the Jerry of Friday evening. 'Aren't any of them married? Are there no women at all out there?'

I waited for his reply, wondering what it was he had *really* said to Greg Tarrant about the new female arrival as to the reason why *she* was not *Mr Tarrant's* type.

'Oh, yes. Some of them are, of course.'

'How do they live? Under canvas?'

'Nick does. They all have to stay pretty mobile, you know. Under canvas or in straw rondavels knocked up by the Minzandan field staff. A few of the married ones trail caravans behind their Land-Rovers; those who can afford 'em. But those with children — their wives and kids stay here in Chundi and the men come in on their free weekends. There's the question of school, you see.'

Children, I found myself thinking, as I crossed to my rondavel, could in fact pose no end of problems beyond the confines of Dora's 'semi-detached-with-the-school-and-supermarket-not-too-far-away'. I wondered why it had not occurred to me before.

Take myself, for instance. I had been four. Had my mother remained in Minzanda she would have had to leave with me for Chundi, or one of the few other towns in Minzanda that had boasted a school in those far-off days, within a year or so at most. And my father had resigned his post with Government, so there would be no free accommodation forthcoming. And what about money? If he made no find of diamonds of any real value, what would they — we — have lived on? Indeed, what had my father been living on all these years? I knew little about the subject, but I could not believe that the revenue from an occasional handful of microscopic, poor-quality industrial stones could be all that great.

My mind became so exercised with the complexity of the problems which must have faced my mother twenty-five years ago, and which I in my ignorance had never even considered until now, that it was some time before I realised with dismay that I had forgotten to ask

Jerry the all-important question of how to get hold of Nick.

I could scarcely ring him back. I was not quite sure why, except that there had been that difference in his manner over the phone that I had found slightly daunting after his casual friendliness of Friday evening. He had been more formal in his office on Saturday, it was true, but —

No, there had been something different then, too. There were those odd looks he had given me when I asked about my father's possible diamond finds. Then there was Nick, who had been so casually and informally helpful, and yet had made no attempt to make contact with me again.

Of course, he could have called at Blake's on Sunday and found me out. In that case, though, would he not have left a message?

But Chundi, after all, was not London. The receptionist would tell me where I could find him.

It was only a little way to walk, the

kindly black receptionist assured me. Down this very road and over the railway crossing I would see the group of buildings on my left. There were pens for sick animals at the back and I was sure to hear them.

Not for the first time I toyed with the idea of hiring a car as I trudged along in the heat of the morning. There were no shops here, with arcades or awnings to give shade, so that apart from the occasional wayside tree I was in full sunlight all the way. A few Africans on bicycles passed me from time to time, mostly khaki-clad messengers upon their errands, and groups of turbaned women with their babies strapped across their backs or toddlers clutching their long, vividly-coloured skirts paused in their gossiping to eye me curiously as I went by.

But if I were leaving Chundi in a day or so there would be no point in hiring a car for so short a time; or would there? I was still undecided when I reached the green-washed Government building that, according to a plaque beside the main door, housed the Veterinary, Game and Tstetse Control Division, Rural Development Section.

I could, indeed, hear the animals. Finding the main entrance a little intimidating for me in my hot and wilting condition, I wandered around the side of the building in the general direction of the intermittent barking and squealing that rent the silence, and found a green-painted, half-open door set into the stuccoed wall.

A strong animal smell, mingled with disinfectant, assailed my nostrils as I passed through into a rectangular courtyard surrounded on three sides by a series of small structures resembling chicken coops. The concrete runs were separately fenced, and in the far corner I saw that a netting roof had been attached. I thought at once of Dora's kitten and crossed towards it to take a closer look. It contained, however, not cats, but a lone small, disconsolate-looking monkey.

The fourth side of the courtyard was the back of the building itself. Four or five doors stood open wide, and white-coated Minzandan staff moved purposefully back and forth among the benches against the wall, where half-a-dozen or so people — mostly women — sat nursing baskets or clutching dog's leads and endeavouring worriedly to calm their nervous charges. It was obviously surgery time.

'Mrs Benson. Rabies injection, isn't it? This way, please.' A white-coated young Minzandan appeared in one of the doorways and beckoned to a waiting woman.

I walked a little apprehensively past the row of waiting people, trying to persuade myself that there could not possibly be any rabid dogs among the leashed animals, while I sought in vain among the assistants for someone to ask about Nick; but in vain.

They were not unfriendly; just very busy or preoccupied. As I moved towards one of the doors a hefty

Minzandan staggered out carrying an enormous — and quite unconscious — red setter in his arms. He smiled at me in thanks as I stepped back hurriedly, and made his way across the yard towards one of the coops or kennels. As I hesitated, a waiting woman smiled up at me and shuffled along the bench to make room.

I thanked her but shook my head and went towards the next door. This opened upon a longish passage, I saw, with several doors opening off at either side.

There obviously had to be more than one vet in evidence, or what happened while Nicholas Locke was out of town? In any case, did he take surgery duty whilst in Chundi? I did not know. The young Minzandan was almost certainly one of the qualified staff. If I hovered in the passageway he might reappear and I could ask him. If he did not, I would go outside and wait on one of the benches. At least they were in the shade.

One of the inner doors was slightly

open upon what appeared to be a small laboratory. On the far side of the room another door stood ajar, though I could see nothing of the interior. I could, however, hear men's voices.

After hesitating for a moment I knocked. It was a faint, timid sort of knock, I suppose, for the voices continued. A little nervously I edged into the room, intending them to hear my footsteps, but my sandals made little sound on the gleaming brown linoleum.

I was about to give the usual cough when I heard Jerry Driscoll's voice.

' — just thought I ought to mention it, that's all. You haven't seen her since Friday, have you?'

'No.' It was Nick. 'I rang through to Blake's yesterday, thinking she might be at a loose end and a bit lonely, but she was out, so I left it. But, damn it all, Jerry, she could just have been thinking up ways of finding him, couldn't she?'

'Or the diamonds?' I did not much like the sound of Jerry's laugh. 'Look,

Nick, how much trouble has she ever taken to find her father before this? Obviously none.'

'No-o. That's true. But — '

'Then we write to her, and out she comes post-haste. And the minute she gets inside my office she starts chatting me up about the old man's diamond finds. Made me think a bit. After all, if it really is concern about her old man that's brought her out here, what the hell's been keeping her up to now?'

I put my hands over my burning cheeks and backed away towards the outer door. As I pressed my fingers into my ears I could hear my heart thumping. My mouth felt sick and dry. Too stricken to hear more, I groped behind me for the door, and Nick's voice became audible once more. I stood transfixed.

' — too good to be true. That London look alone. If ever a girl had it, she has. What does she do — modelling?'

'No. P.A. to the boss of some big firm

of architects, according to my spies. But, Nick — '

'She didn't look *real*, you know. Up at the airport. When I put out my hand to shake hers I almost expected to come up against a glass wall, or cellophane wrapping.' He began to laugh. It was a rueful sort of laugh, however, 'Oh, well, at least it was nice looking, anyway. She has the sort of bone structure a cousin of mine back in Edinburgh would like to paint. Those angles and hollows. Ha! Well, thanks anyway, Jerry. Don't worry, I won't get involved.'

'Well, it's Callow's wishes that matter, after all. He engaged me to trace her and I have. What'll you do now, Nick?'

'Ask around.' He laughed again, the same brief little bark. 'See if anybody here's seen Kelly, for a start.' A pause. 'I suppose Callow's on his last legs out there somewhere — or thinks he is. After chasing after his pot of gold, or diamonds, rather, for a quarter of a century, he's finally discovered it was all nothing more than a dream, and he's got nothing left. His wife left him — probably a laquered sort of bird like this one, who couldn't take it — so he has only one thing left to dream about, and that's finding his daughter before he fades out. Poor devil. Poor *devil*.'

Jerry grunted in agreement. 'I'd better get back. I've an appointment with old man Fosdyke at ten and it's a sixty-mile drive into Chundi from his place, so I'd better not keep him waiting. See you, Nick. I'll go out this way if I may. There's a posse of women and animals out at the back, and a hell of a pong.'

It was not until I let my breath out in relief that I was at least to be spared a confrontation with Jerry Driscoll, that I realised I had been holding it until my ribs ached. Silently I pulled the door further ajar and stepped out into the corridor; straight into the path of the Minzandan vet.

He beamed at me. 'Can I help you?'

I stared back at him, quite unable to

speak. A moment ago I had been seeking him — or someone; now, all I wanted was to escape.

An expression of concern crossed his face. 'Madam is faint?' He tut-tutted. 'It is very hot just now. You would like some water? A seat in the shade?'

He took my elbow as I struggled to find words, and at that very moment the door swung wide behind me, and Nick Locke appeared.

'Hello, there,' he said. His voice was as cheerful, the tone as friendly and casual as ever. How did he do it? Then I realised that he was not, after all, aware of my inadvertent eavesdropping. 'Looking for me?'

'Ah.' The Minzandan looked relieved, but still eyed me searchingly. 'The lady has felt the heat, I think.'

'In that case, Joseph, I think she'll be better in here. There's a bit of an assortment of smells at the back, wouldn't you say? Come and sit down, Emma. Did you walk from Blake's?'

Joseph grinned at him, then at me.

'I'll leave you in good hands then, Madam. Shall I bring some water, Nick?'

'No.' I put out a hand towards him. 'No water. I'm — I'll be fine. It's just the heat, honestly.' I had never been so grateful for an excuse.

The African nodded and wandered away, whistling tunelessly. I started to follow him, but I was too slow. In his turn Nick took my arm and led me through to the inner room, where an enormous desk and two or three chairs indicated it as Nick's office.

He pushed me into one of the chairs and crossed to a small fridge in the corner.

'Here,' he said, pouring liquid into a tumbler. 'It's only soda water, but it'll help.' He stood watching me while I took the glass and began to sip.

'Half a mile at least in the full sun with no hat, and you not used to it,' he remarked reprovingly. 'That *was* a silly thing to do.'

My hand was trembling so that my

teeth rattled against the glass as I drank. He reached and took it from me and stood with it, waiting.

'A little more,' he said at last. 'Come on, now.' He knelt and held the tumbler against my lips, tilting it at just the right angle, in the way I had seen mothers do with young children, for me to drink. Something in the innate, unfailing kindness of this giant of a man made my eyes smart, and a lump rose in my throat so that I could not swallow.

Anybody, I thought; anybody and everybody, would be grist to his mill. Small black kittens, swaying, half-drunken strangers bearing messages, too tall English girls walking with heads held high because they were too proud to let anyone know how much they hated being as tall as most men, taller than many, and head and shoulders above almost every member of their own sex —

'Enough?' He set the glass down on the desk. 'Now just sit quietly for a moment, then I'll get you some tea.'

I was not, however, Emma Callow for nothing, and I was already beginning to recover. I had blinked away my tears. 'You're too big to cry, Emma; tall girls don't cry — ' and the lump in my throat was melting, while I reminded myself that tall girls didn't faint, either, to be scooped up in the arms of attractive males, unless they wanted to make themselves a laughing-stock.

Somehow, the thought restored my equanimity. The vision of even Nick trying to manoeuvre my unconscious form through the narrow doorway, size sevens feet first, while trying to get through himself, head and shoulders crouched beneath the lintel, evoked such a strong desire to giggle that it must have shown in my face.

'Feeling better, are you? That's the stuff. Like some tea now?'

I almost refused, then remembered my mission, and nodded instead.

By the time we sat opposite each other, tea tray on the desk between us, I was my own woman again, and able, even, to review Jerry Driscoll's comments a little more objectively.

After all, he did not know me. He could not know that I had spent the last eleven years living my own life, holding down a job that had become progressively more responsible and onerous, and that those years had given me a business woman's approach to any problem. He could not know that diamonds, hypothetical or real, industrial or of gem quality, held interest for me only as a means of finding my father; that not once had I even thought of them as *diamonds*.

I had wanted him to be still searching for them in the same place because it would have made finding him that much easier, and so in my typical, one-track-minded way, I had waded straight into the subject of the wretched things without a thought as to how it might sound to a stranger.

What had he called me? Cover-girl and glossy. He must be mad. Of course, Dora Bannister had said that the man-woman ratio was three to one. That must be the explanation. To a sex-starved man any woman might look like a cross between Elizabeth Taylor and Sophia Loren. And perhaps Greg Tarrant, the hunter, was so sex-starved in his tsetse corridor that Jerry had feared for my virtue.

As for Nick and his glass walls and cellophane wrappings —

That, of course, was partly my own fault. I *had* become too self-contained and unapproachable in my manner over the years, as I well knew. I also knew that it was my own particular form of self-defence. My mother had seen in me a certain kind of woman, and events had a way of proving my mother right in most cases, as I had already observed; and not without bitterness at that.

'Better now?'

I had been so deep in my thoughts that he startled me. He saw it and smiled. 'You were miles away.'

I managed to smile back at him.

Strange, how companionable he could make a long silence seem. He didn't mind, or grow restless or bored. He simply waited.

'Not as many miles as I plan to be.'

'Oh? Thinking of going home?' His face became an expressionles mask, as though he were hiding something. Relief, probably.

I shook my head vehemently. 'Not till I find my father. That's why I want to come with you.'

His eyes widened. 'To the valley? My dear girl, that's simply not possible. I don't think you quite realise — '

'Please. Please listen to me. It has become of the utmost importance to me to see and speak to my father before he dies. I don't remember him, you see, and I've got to know, now, while he's alive, what he's like, and I'm afraid there may not be much time left.'

'Emma — '

'I'll do everything you tell me to do. I won't get in your way; I promise. You'll have to tell me what kind of things to take because I don't know, but I'll go out and buy them if you'll give me a list, and I'll — '

'Emma.' His tone was as quiet and deliberate as ever, yet something about it brought me to a halt. I watched as he rose and crossed the little room to the doorway through which Jerry Driscoll must have made his escape, put his head through and peered at something on the outer wall. He came back and sat down. Then he pointed to the whirring fan on the top of the filing cabinet beside him.

'Today's temperature — shade temperature — according to the thermometer on that wall out there, is ninety-five. It will probably rise to ninety-seven or so by two o'clock. And the humidity's rising all the time. Rain's already fallen in the east.' He leaned forward, as he had done in Blake's on my first evening, his silver-grey eyes holding mine.

'When I left the valley on Friday morning it was already ninety-seven. It

147

would almost certainly top the hundred mark by two o'clock.' He flapped a hand at the fan. 'We don't have those little luxuries under canvas, you know. And as soon as we have a shower or two the humidity can rise to as much as eighty per cent.

'Chundi itself is a non-malarious area; has been for years. The Municipal Authorities are very, very careful to keep it so. Do you know that every drain in every building within the town area is inspected every week by anti-malaria staff and treated, that it is an offence to leave stagnant water about in a bucket or container, and that the anti-malaria employees will kick over and spray any they see?

'And yet, here and there, now and then, people still manage to contract malaria. They drive down to the river for a whiff of air or an hour's fishing around sundown perhaps, or — oh, any number of things. Anyway, it happens. It's rare now, but it happens.

'In the valley, however — ' He

frowned in the way I had seen him do, in that earnest fashion of his, so that a deep crease appeared between his brows. 'That's another story. Then there are the snakes. Even here in town one rarely goes through a rainy season without discovering at least one — a small cobra, perhaps — somewhere in the garden. One's garden boy is usually resourceful enough to clout it over the head with a stick or a brick and that's that.'

I swallowed, then said as steadily as I could: 'But *you* do it. You go out there, and you survive.'

'It's my job. Then there are scorpions. Ever seen a scorpion, Emma? About that long.' He opened his hand, wide. 'Ugly creatures. Even I can't love 'em. Darkish-brown. Tail curled behind them. Move a bit as though they were on miniature stilts.'

'But you said there were women out there.'

'That's right. Sometimes; not all the time; and now that school's started there may be none. Anyway, they were born in Africa, most of them. They're used to it. Take it for granted. Now you; you're a city girl. You're — oh, look at you.'

'What's wrong with me?'

He sighed. 'Nothing. Nothing at all. Far from it. For where you live and the kind of live you're used to, you are probably the most perfect specimen I'll ever see. But — Well, damn it. That hair of yours, for example. How often d'you have it washed, visit a hairdresser? How long d'you think it would stay like that in the valley?' He shook his head at me almost wonderingly.

A perfect specimen, I reflected sourly. Of what? An Amazonian survival, no doubt. 'I'll manage,' I told him firmly. 'I won't worry you, I promise.'

'And your laundry. Used to rinsing out your bras and panties every day, no doubt, and hanging 'em up to dry. Well, you won't hang them out there, unless you want putsi fly.'

'Want *what*?'

'Putsi fly. It's an insect that has an endearing habit of laying its eggs on clothing hanging in the sun. So unless you iron, thoroughly, every single stitch before you wear it (and I can't see you giving the domestic staff — who are all males — your most intimate garments to be gone over with a charcoal iron that'll probably be far too hot for them anyway), the eggs will hatch out in the warmth of the body — '

'Hatch out into what?' He was exaggerating, of course. All the same —

'Maggots, sort of, I suppose you'd call them. They will then dig themselves comfortably in under your skin — '

'Stop it. I could never have believed you'd be so — so revolting. Besides — '

His eyes widened. 'You don't believe me? I've a book on 'em somewhere. I'll find it in a minute, and you can read it for yourself. Very common in Africa, putsi fly. I've had a couple myself. One on the thigh and the other in the small of my back. You take a plaster dressing and a spot of vaseline — '

'I don't want to know, thank you.' It couldn't be true. Could it?

'No? Oh, you should. You'll need all the tips you can get if you're going bush-whacking. Then there's buffalo bean, of course.' A dreamy look came into his eyes. 'All over the place, buffalo bean, in the valley.'

My determination not to ask him, under any circumstances, what a buffalo bean was, or did, battled with my curiosity and lost. 'What will *that* do; eat me alive?' I inquired sarcastically.

'It feels a bit like that, yes. Not in the way you mean, I imagine. It's a fattish, browny-black bean, furry and quite large. A vine, like an ordinary bean. Every one is full of itching powder; murderous stuff, and I'm not joking. It works its way inside socks, or the lace-holes of boots, or you may brush against it inadvertently with your bare arm.'

'So it makes you itch. Like a nettle in England.'

'No, Emma. Not like a nettle. Nothing like a nettle at all. The discomfort is indescribable, I can tell you. I've seen sufferers from this stuff scratch till they bled.' He sighed.

'Look, Emma.' He waved at the half-empty glass. 'You nearly fainted just now, just from the heat here in Chundi.'

Not from the heat, I thought savagely. From the shock of seeing myself as others see me; two young men who had, I believed, even begun to like me.

'I never faint,' I told him coldly. 'I have never fainted in my life. I — I didn't feel like breakfast, that was all.' It was the only lie I could think of on the spur of the moment.

'As for snakes and mosquitoes, and scorpions, I can weather them if you can. I'm not pretending they won't scare me, but I'll manage. Take me with you. Please.'

'You'll be begging me to bring you back before the first night's out.' He thrust a hand through his hair. 'Look, I've got to make you see. For instance,

153

you aren't expecting plumbing, are you? I assure you there isn't any. There are spiders the like of which you've never seen, among other things. Hunting spiders, for instance. We call 'em rain spiders too, because they appear when the rains are due; just about now, in fact.' He spread his thumb and forefinger to their widest extent. 'About that long. Cockroach-brown. Long bodies; not round. Move like lightning. If you aim to kill you have to whack out about a foot ahead of where they're running. They'll terrify you.'

He watched me while he spoke, as though awaiting my reaction.

'Oh, and ticks, of course. And leeches, and termites. They'd eat the very legs of the chair from under your — er — you, if we didn't use metal frames.'

I thought of the thatch above my bed, and of all the beastly creatures my imagination had peopled it with, and drew a deep breath. 'I promise you,' I repeated, 'I'll stick it out till I find him.'

154

There was a long silence, which instinctively I knew I must not break, while he studied me.

I actually saw the glint touch his eyes; and recognised it at once. I did not possess a younger brother without having learnt a thing or two. It brightened as they rested first on my hair, my impeccably manicured nails and untanned hands, and wandered back again, speculatively, to my hair. Did he think, I wondered with a touch of malice, to see a navy-blue parting appear within a week? In that at least he would be disappointed.

When his eyes met mine at last I knew I had won, if only because the gleam was more pronounced than ever. It was a gleam of unadulterated, unholy mischief. It might be fun at that, it seemed to be saying, just to see how you make out; and at least you can never say I didn't warn you.

He picked up a pad and pencil from the desk. 'All right,' he said. 'Here's what you'll need,' and began to write.

7

The sun was up, but only just, when we left Chundi behind two mornings later. The air was as clear as crystal, and quite the sweetest I had ever breathed.

I have never regarded a Land-Rover as being in the least birdlike, yet as we forged ahead across the rapidly rising terrain it seemed almost as though we were, in fact, flying.

Not that we were travelling fast; a Land-Rover being built for reliability under all conditions rather than speed. There was simply a sort of exhilaration in leaving Chundi not only behind, but below us, so soon.

I should not have been surprised, I suppose. Nick had, after all, referred to Chundi as lying in a basin, and a basin must have sides. And a lip, of course.

'My ears are crackling,' I said at one point. 'Why is that? Are we so high?'

'Not so very, yet. But you know, so much of inland Africa is well above sea level. Even Chundi lies at three thousand feet or thereabouts. So that when you *do* start to climb you can feel it. Just hold your nose and have a good swallow. See those hills ahead? We shall be going through them to reach the valley, and then — '

'Through, not over?'

'Not exactly. The road's metalled a few miles ahead, and it stays that way until we come down on the other side. Quite a decent bit of engineering really, you'll see. They cut a road *through*, or between, mountainous terrain like this. You find them in a great many parts of Africa. There's a rather spectacular one in South Africa not far south of the Rhodesian border, only in that case they've tunnelled it in. Very tricky terrain indeed, and a wonderful job. When you come out at the other side you feel a bit the way Jesus must have felt when the Devil led him to the top of a high place.'

I gazed ahead at the approaching mountains. 'You called them hills,' I said reproachfully. 'I'm positive that peak's higher than Snowdon.'

'Oh, it is. But then, it starts higher, if you see what I mean. Here's the escarpment now, coming up. And here's the tarmac, thank the Lord.'

'Escarpment? That's a sort of pass, isn't it?'

'That's exactly what it is. A pass through the mountains. Don't worry, it's quite safe. Though I don't think I'd have cared to do it before it was metalled, the way the pioneers must have had to.'

And now my ears really crackled, while the road twisted and turned back on itself, and climbed higher and higher. In the back I could hear Thomas, Nick's factotum, slithering into a firmer position amid the miscellany of gear while the roadside fell away alarmingly, first on Nick's side, then on mine.

Then Nick swung the Land-Rover

round the final bend, drew up on the side of the road — on the very edge, it seemed, of nowhere — and said: 'There you are. That's it,' and grinned at me while I gaped.

From where we sat the valley floor lay like a vast golden-brown carpet far below us, dotted here and there with palest green and disappearing into a purple blur in the distance.

It took quite a long moment for me to realise that what I was actually looking down upon was a carpet of treetops; the earth was barely visible at all, save for the road that curved away below and scored a wavy line long the valley until it disappeared amid the blur.

'It's magnificent,' I whispered, awed. 'All that space. All that — nothingness.'

Nick laughed. 'Yes. In Britain it's always split up into fields and fences, or whatever, even when you do come upon a view of nothing, as you put it. And in the Highlands, where it's lonely enough, heaven knows, the mountains hem one in. I think these vast areas with limitless horizons must be peculiar to Africa; and parts of America, of course.'

'But it looks as though there's nothing down there — nothing at all. It's like the end of the world — frightening, somehow.'

Nick started the engine and edged the Land-Rover gently back on to the crown of the road. 'Oh, no. There's plenty down there. It's true that all you can see are treetops, but there's plenty underneath. Wild game, small villages, game reserve, rest camps, farms — pretty widely scattered, but they're there — a mission or two —'

'It's fantastic. It's — I'm glad I saw it, like that.' We were descending rapidly now and my ears began to crackle again.

We left the road soon afterwards to follow a rough, deeply-rutted track among the trees. 'How d'you know where they'll be?' I asked, marvelling at how one could find anybody — or anything — in an area as vast as that which I had seen from above.

'I get my marching orders from Chundi a couple of days before I leave.'

'How do *they* know?'

He laughed. 'Well, they're the bosses. They give the directives. We work a certain area each season according to where game's been sighted.' He seemed to sense my bewilderment. 'It's a very large area, you know. Runs parallel to the eastern border. Most of Minzanda's best agricultural land lies beyond the corridor, and the ranches cover anything from eight to fifteen thousand acres.

'We have twelve camps scattered about the corridor. They're all given code names for radio purposes. At the moment we're heading for Kudu, to which I'm assigned for the next three weeks.'

'Who'll be there besides — us?'

'Let's see. One tsetse field officer — that's the white hunter — and twenty Minzandan hunters. Five or six camp scouts — and cookboys and such — that's about it.'

'No — women?'

'I rather think not. Greg Tarrant isn't married. Look.'

I should never have seen it. Amid the grey background of tree trunks, with the gloom of limitless bush behind it, the elephant was, for all its size, all but invisible to any but a trained eye such as Nick's.

And it was certainly the most enormous creature I had ever seen. We were moving very slowly — too slowly, I suddenly discovered, for my peace of mind — as we passed it. The creature stood eyeing us, trunk lowered and massive ears gently flapping. It was less than five yards away from my elbow.

I was frightened, and more than thankful, when Nick, loitering (rather unnecessarily, I felt) for me to get a closer look, accelerated until it was a comfortable distance behind us.

But I was also lost in wonder, and conscious of the thrill that had swept through me. Never again would the sight of an animal behind bars mean anything to me, I felt. 'An elephant,' I kept muttering. 'A real live elephant, just standing there, on the side of the road.'

'Very common. Very common indeed. Nothing out of the way at all.' He stole a look at my face and began to laugh. 'This is Africa, Emma, not Clapham Common.'

'Would he have gone for us?'

'Only if he was feeling peeved about something.' It did not seem much in the way of a reassuring reply.

'How would we have known if he was?' I think I was still feeling a little breathless from the very *closeness* of the thing, and accordingly irritable about it.

'Oh, we'd have known. His trunk would be well up, his ears flapping madly and his eyes glaring. And he'd have been making the most blood-curdling trumpeting sound.' He turned the Land-Rover expertly off the track and on to an even worse one — no more than two rutted lines through the bush — and added: 'Thirsty yet?'

'Gasping.'

'Put your hand outside your door. There's a water bag hanging around there somewhere. Paper cups just behind you. Just haul it in — that's it. I'll have some too.'

The water was surprisingly cold, but the flavour of wet canvas could not be denied. Nick, emptying his cup with alacrity, grinned at me.

'It's an acquired taste, like smoked salmon,' he said.

I took another swig, and grimaced.

'Drink it up. Every drop. That's water, my girl. *Water*. The most precious thing we're carrying, apart possibly from my Winchester .375. More precious than gold — or diamonds.'

We stopped at last, at a clearing, where several African camp staff idled and gossiped amid a huddle of straw rondavels and a kind of oblong canvas tent such as I had seen only on films. There was a glowing fire set between piled stones, with a metal sheet or tray laid across. Various pots bubbled on the tray while one of the Africans tended it. They did not seem in the least surprised to see us, and several hurried towards us as we approached, beaming a welcome.

'Coffee, Jacob,' said Nick to one of them. 'Thomas. Fetch our grub.' He smiled at me. 'We try not to raid each other's larders.'

'Oh. But isn't this it? Aren't we there?'

'Heavens, no. This is Buffalo, Jefferson's camp. Ours — Tarrant's — is another forty miles or so. But you must be hungry. I know I am. 'Any vension going, Jacob? We'll have some of that. One thing there's never any shortage of out here,' he added to me.

'Plenty, boss. Shall I cut some?'

'Rather.' Nick helped me down from the Land-Rover, eyeing my denim-clad legs and safari-booted feet approvingly.

'At least you're dressed for the part.' I fancied, however, that the glint still lurked in his eyes.

'Where *is* Mr — er — Jefferson?' I asked while we ate.

'Out doing his job.'

'Oh — yes. What does he do with — whatever he kills?'

'Oh, he's only after the big stuff. The African hunters take the light game; bush buck, kudu, pig. They haul the kill on to the side of the road — or track — to be picked up by Land-Rover.' He grinned at me. 'We leave the bigger stuff where it falls and let the chaps climb in. They quite like elephant.'

'Where will they be?'

'Oh, somewhere within a ten-or-so-mile radius of camp, depending on the game. A Land-Rover takes them out in the morning and drops them off.'

'Do they hunt all day?'

'Yes, but not when it's as hot as this. They'll be back about two or so. But we must be on our way before then. I brought him some fresh vegetables so we'd better get them out. Come and help me.'

As we clambered back into our seats and began the last lap of our journey I said: 'What do you *do* about things like that? Vegetables, I mean. And butter, and —'

'Yes, well. It's a bit difficult. Fresh foods are out for these chaps — apart from meat of course. There's all the venison one could wish for, all the time. Apart from that most of their stuff has to come out of tins. They bring out a supply of fresh vegetables to last a day or so, but that's all they can do. We're a bit luckier.'

'We are?'

'I travel with a paraffin deep-freezer — that's it at the back, wrapped in sacking. Have to, for the blood samples and such. So I tuck away a spot of bacon and butter and so on, and we'll be eating fresh vegetables for about a fortnight.' He flashed me a grin. 'So you see, from the food point of view, things won't be too bad.'

'Will there be any water where we're going?'

Nick considered. 'Depends on the state of the river nearby. I think there just might be.'

'Are all the camps near rivers?'

'Well, yes. That's one of the considerations. But if they dry up, as on my last trip' — he shrugged — 'that's it.'

I wanted to ask about washing or bathing, but did not dare.

'If there's water in the river will I be able to go in? For a dip?'

'In this one? We-ell. It's bound to be low.'

'Will there be crocodiles?'

'No. At least — they tend to hug the perennial rivers, but, of course, you never can tell. Crocs travel overland, too, you know. Let's wait and see, shall we?'

We drove along in silence for a while. My back ached with the constant jolting, and my posterior felt as though I'd been riding a mule over the Andes.

Because of this, and our early start,

and the long, hot afternoon, I must have fallen asleep, incredible as it seemed to me later.

It was the late afternoon sun in my eyes that woke me. We were travelling along a broad — and quite good — dirt road across a ridge of ground that gave a surprisingly wide view in all directions. The entire vista was bathed in an amber glow that was strangely beautiful; even the anthills seemed touched with gold, and deep purple shadows lay between the trees on either side. Ahead of us, in the middle distance, a long, low hill was silhouetted against the sky-line.

'I must have dozed,' I muttered incredulously, massaging my neck with a dust-grimed hand. 'Where are we? What's this road? Are we nearly there?'

'We're nearly there; we're in the corridor; this is just one of the main roads through — they're kept pretty well graded as far as possible for the hunting — and there's your Diamond Hill in the distance. Any more questions?'

He gave me a sideways grin that was as good-humoured as ever. But the lines between his eyes and at the corners of his mouth were more pronounced, his thick, straight hair untidier than ever so that a strand that had begun to turn silver-grey hung low across his brow, and I realised with a stab of guilt how bone-tired he must be.

'I could at least have stayed awake to keep you company,' I said remorsefully, glancing behind me to where Thomas, stretched full length amid the paraphernalia, was snoring softly.

'Not at all. I could have dozed myself, almost. This thing,' he tapped the wheel affectionately, 'knows its way as well as any horse.'

I laughed. 'Will they be expecting us?'

'They'd better be. I've got an aching void where my tum ought to be. How about you?'

He turned off the road as he spoke and drove across a rough track between the trees. 'The camp's just ahead — see the edge of the clearing?'

There was another sign — of which we had passed many on the way — saying starkly: 'Don't start fires' with a similar injunction in the vernacular beneath it, then we emerged into a wide, cleared space and a tall, thickset man in a khaki shirt and shorts left the group at the camp and came towards us.

He reached my door almost before Nick had time to brake, flung it open and held out his hands. Before I was aware of his intention he had lifted me down as effortlessly as though I were a child, instead of ten stone of full-grown womanhood, and set me on the ground. 'Miss Callow,' he said. 'Now, isn't that nice?' He shot out a huge hand and gripped mine. 'Greg Tarrant, and very much at your service, my dear. Hello, Nick.'

'H'm. Wondered when you were going to notice me.' Nick strode to the back of the Land-Rover, leaned inside and shook Thomas vigorously by the shoulder. 'Wakey, wakey. Come on, Thomas. Let's get unloaded while we can still see what we're doing.'

Greg Tarrant waved a massive arm in the direction of the scouts and camp staff, and in an astonishingly short time the tents were erected, camp beds set up, deep-freezer working, and equipment unloaded and in its place.

'What's for dinner?' asked Nick. 'We're starving. And how's the river?'

'Low, but still wet, thank God. There's a nice bit of venison roasting.' He caught my eye, his face deadpan. 'Like venison?'

Nick laughed shortly. 'She will, before she's through. Or starve.' He picked up his box of tricks, as he called it, in one hand, reached for the Winchester with the other, and disappeared into his tent.

Already somebody had brought hot water to mine in a brimming four-gallon petrol can with the top cut off, and poured it into a galvanised bath of a size in which a buxom two-year-old might comfortably splash around.

Despite this restrictive circumstance, I had never enjoyed a bath more. I stood, crouched, and swished about it it as though I had not bathed for a week, and may not bath again for another, telling myself as I soaped away that one took altogether too many of civilisation's amenities far too much for granted.

It was still not dark when I emerged, and though one of the camp staff was preparing two or three Tilley lamps, none were lit. I walked across the rising ground of the clearing, away from the African hunters' quarters and the babel of their incessant chatter and laughter, until I stood on the far ridge where I could stare across the expanse of scrub and open ground towards Diamond Hill.

It was, quite suddenly, astonishingly quiet; it was also breathtakingly lovely. The ground undulated, and I could see the glint of water where the river — very low in its bed — flowed past below the camp. Everything was bathed in a clear, pale golden light, with Diamond Hill darkened to an almost inky black against the delicate, duck-egg blue of the evening sky.

It was a strange shape; a long, barrow of a hill with cone-like peaks rising out of it at irregular intervals. In the foreground a gleam of light from the sun's after-glow caught the corrugated-iron roofs of a group of buildings, half-hidden by a stand of conifers.

'That's your limit,' said a voice behind me. 'No further.' It was Greg Tarrant, and as I turned I saw Nick coming up behind him.

'No wandering about here, Emma. It's dangerous, in case you hadn't grasped the fact.'

'I wasn't — I wouldn't have gone any further. It's nearly dark — '

'Even in the daytime. We shall be away at 6.30 tomorrow, and you and the domestics have the camp to yourselves. You stay in the camp. Understand?'

'I — well, yes.' I felt irrationally annoyed. I don't know quite what else I had expected. Now that I thought about it, it was obvious that I could not be allowed to go with them. And yet I had come to find my father; something I was unlikely to do sitting on a canvas chair in the shade of a tent flap. I really was, I thought dejectedly, all kinds of a fool, and it was a conclusion which patient, long-suffering Nicholas Locke must have reached quite a while ago. It was nice of him not to show it.

'What's that group of buildings over there?' I pointed.

'Mission,' said Greg.

'Leprosarium,' said Nick simultaneously. Greg glared at him. 'It's a mission primarily,' he insisted. 'Why talk to Miss Callow about that kind of thing? She doesn't want to know — '

'She may not *want* to know, but it's still there.' He took my arm. 'Come on. They're lighting the lamps. It's not safe now outside the perimeter.' I noticed, for the first time, the rifle tucked under his arm, barrel lowered in the approved manner.

'We leave a rifle in the camp,' he said, following my glance. 'It will be loaded and placed in your tent. Not that the chaps who stay behind would be much good with it. Amos — Greg's boy — is the only one who can shoot with any sort of accuracy at all. Still, it'll be here, that's the thing.'

'We'll leave him behind,' said Greg reassuringly. 'And nothing's — er — likely to come in this direction. Nothing big, that is.'

'Why?'

'We-ell. Ground's too open for 'em to actually choose it, and they smell humans a mile away. Besides, we head 'em away from the camp whenever we sight anything. Naturally.'

'Yes, I see.' It didn't sound altogether reassuring, but it was far too late in the day for me to say so. I approached the glow of the lamps and the dancing flames of the fire gratefully, a stalwart male on either side.

'Ever handled one of these?' Nick tapped the .375 with a finger tip. I shook my head. 'No, but my stepfather — '

'Ah, well. Not to worry. You'll be all right.' He pulled a canvas chair further away from a hanging Tilley around which an unbelievable variety of insects already fluttered. 'There you are. Gin and tonic, or sherry? Dinner in about half-an-hour.'

I laughed. 'Oh, sherry, please,' and honestly thought he was joking until the tumbler was placed in my hand. Greg had wandered over to the African hunters' quarters, and I could see him in the glow from their fire, collecting something from each of them and handing it over to Amos.

'What's he doing?'

'Collecting their rifles. He locks 'em away every evening.' Nick frowned. 'Earlier than this, as a rule. Probably our arrival put him off. He's packing them away in that box, you see? Then a couple of them will carry it over to his tent, just in case anybody gets trigger-happy during the night.'

'You mean — do they get drunk?'

'Not if we know it. And they're a good lot, really. But,' his teeth flashed in the firelight, 'they brew some really fierce concoctions at times, you know. Make a Highlander's illicit whisky taste like mother's milk. Then all it needs is for somebody to start an argument — '

'But what with, for heaven's sake? I mean, what do they brew it *from*?'

'Whatever they can lay hands on. Cane spirit's a favourite. Or there's a pretty fierce opaque beer they're fond of.'

'And you — the field officer allows —?'

'Oh, Emma. Of course not. Not officially. But we're not here all day. Anyway, it doesn't happen often, and Greg's are a first-class lot. But it's been *known* to happen, so the powers-that-be have decreed a lock-up of all .270s — light game arms — on return to camp. It's better than letting 'em kill each other over some trivial difference of opinion instead of just giving each other a sock on the jaw. Always have thought that's what's wrong in America, basically. Too many firearms, too readily available.'

We watched the two Africans — Amos and one of the hunters — carry the box across to Greg's tent, waiting for the white hunter to return to his beer.

'He's a long time,' said Nick at last. 'What's he doing?'

We heard Greg's voice raised briefly, as though in altercation, then he lifted an enormous arm and beckoned in our direction. He was calling something, but it was impossible to hear him above the babel from the Africans around him. As we approached he came to meet us. 'He's here,' he said. 'He's here, and they never said a word. Would you believe it?'

'*Who*? Who's here?' But even as I asked, I knew.

* * *

'Kelly, of course. Arrived here rolling drunk, so Amos told them, just before we got back to camp. Asked if you'd arrived.' He nodded at Nick. 'They told him you were expected, and that you were bringing a Madam from London with you.'

'But how would they know?' I stared at Greg in disbelief, while I thought; drunk again. How can he know anything? How can a raving alcoholic help?

'They always know.' Greg smiled at me briefly. 'Bush telegraph. Never fails.'

'Where did they put him?' asked Nick.

Greg indicated a straw rondavel beside his own tent. 'In there, where I stow some of my gear.' We followed him as he strode towards it, Tilley swinging from his hand.

One sees few tramps about the English towns and countryside today, but I suppose I had seen my share of itinerant hippies and drop-outs. Nevertheless, I had never come across anything like the man who lay stretched out on the camp bed inside the rondavel, deep in a profound stupor, it seemed.

As Nick had said, very little of his features were visible beneath the matted hair that covered cheeks, upper lip and chin, to say nothing of the dirty grey mass of the stuff that flowed across his brow and shoulders. He wore what had once been khaki drill safaris; now, apart from their filthy condition, the cuffs and trouser-ends were in tatters, and one of the pockets hung by no more than two or three threads. Most of the buttons were gone, and a couple of ragged shoe-laces held the garment loosely together where holes had appeared in the fabric as the buttons had fallen off.

He wore the kind of safari boot, with the soft, suede-type uppers, that Nick had prescribed for me, and which both he and Greg were wearing. But a black-grimed toenail poked through the cap of one, and the sole was fast parting company with the upper of the other. There were darkish stains on the fabric where the foot had bled, and dried.

One arm lay behind his head, the long, grimed fingers curled as though he had been gripping his scalp in an agony of hangover headache. The other drooped loosely downwards with the fingers almost touching the groundsheeted floor. He was dreadfully emaciated, and in the hot, still air the smell of him was appalling.

I fumbled in the pocket of my denims for a handkerchief, stepping back involuntarily as I did so, at the precise moment that Nick moved towards him. He stood for a few seconds looking down at him, frowning in the way he had when thinking deeply. Then he lifted the drooping arm and held the wrist as though feeling for a pulse. Finally he leaned over the man's face so that his own was almost touching it, while Greg and I watched silently.

Then Nick laid a finger gently on one eyelid and lifted it. 'He's just flat out,' he said at last. 'In a deep sleep.' He was still frowning.

Greg snorted. 'Well, of course he is. You had me thinking he was dead for a moment. Come on, let's get out of here. The smell's enough to knock your hat off.'

'Yes. Better let him sleep it off.' He followed us out, then turned again in the doorway as though for a final look, catching my eye as he did so.

My distaste must have shown in my face. I was ashamed and tried to hide it, but I suppose I was too late. His gaze lingered on me for what was probably no more than a second, but seemed much longer, before he strode away towards the fire.

'We'd better eat,' he said. 'We turn in early here. I have to make radio contact with Chundi at six every morning, and Greg likes to get away by half-past.'

8

I woke before the sun had fully risen: even so, everyone was up and about except myself. I dressed quickly and went out into a scene of organised activity in which everybody seemed to have a job to do — and to be getting on with it — but me.

Greg beamed at me and waved towards the fire. 'There's kidneys,' he said, 'and eggs. What'll you have?'

Even as I stood wondering dubiously whose kidneys they were, so to speak, he was away and across the camp, handing out rifles to the Minzandan hunters and shouting orders to the driver to bring the Land-Rover round, while Nick, radio call completed. strode over and took his breakfast plate from the cook.

'Help yourself,' he said, indicating the coffee-pot. 'And pour one for me, will you?'

It was obviously no moment for small talk, and I did as he asked before accepting a plate of scrambled eggs, kidneys, and — incredibly — a hot, fresh roll from the cook. He saw the surprise in my face and grinned, white teeth flashing.

'Good,' he said. 'Madam try. Daniel make good bread.'

'He does, too.' Nick eyed me over the rim of his cup. Probably waiting for me to enquire regarding the provenance of the kidneys, I decided, and waded into them forthwith. They were delicious.

Still he watched me, the now-familiar glint lurking like silent laughter behind his silvery eyes.

'What are you staring at?' I asked a trifle waspishly.

'Was I staring? I'm sorry.' He shook his head wonderingly. 'I don't quite know why it is, but somehow I always find myself expecting a hidden orchestra to blast forth, or cameras to start clicking, the moment you appear.' He waved a hand about us. 'You know,

Born Free, or *Where No Vultures Fly* — or are you old enough to remember *that* one?'

'I shall be thirty in another five months,' I replied frostily, at which, to my astonishment, he burst out laughing. I glared at him for a moment before grinning back at him reluctantly.

'I'll say this for you.' He held out his cup for a refill. 'You're not like any other woman I've ever met. Always the unexpected. Ninety-nine women out of a hundred would either have said 'No'; or: 'I'm twenty-nine'.'

'I'm also five foot ten in my stockings.'

'Ha. A mere shrimp. Five ten's nothing. I'd change places with you any day. I'm six-four and I've had far more bops on the head than's good for anyone, especially back home. What with door lintels and wealths of olde worlde beams — '

'You'd better not let my stepfather hear you. He's an estate agent.'

'Well, just so long as he stays out of my way.'

We were still grinning at each other when Greg came back for a last coffee. He looked from one to the other of us speculatively. 'Missing all the fun, am I?' He beamed at me. '*You're* a sight for sore eyes in the middle of the sticks first thing in the morning, Miss Callow.'

'Emma. Please.'

'Emma. I really go for a young lady who can look like you *and* laugh at this hour of the day.'

Since I could not remember ever having been up, let alone falling hilariously about, at such an unearthly hour — and had always detested those who were and did — I was at a loss for words, and we stood companionably sipping coffee while the sun's first rays sliced the clearing, and the dawn chorus tailed off around us, until Nick said:

'I looked in on Kelly. He's still out, I'm afraid.'

'Must have had a skinful,' muttered Greg. 'Perhaps he's got his own still. The Irish are as bad as the Scots at that lark.' He eyed Nick mischievously, but Nick refused the bait.

'I've told Thomas to keep an eye out and tell you if he wakes. Also to help him to — er — clean up a bit before you see him.' The last was said quite expressionlessly while he stared into the dregs of his coffee.

'Amos is staying, too.' Greg picked up his .404 and set down his cup. 'If you want anything, just ask.'

'And if you want to take a walk, take Amos with you, *and* the gun,' warned Nick. 'Right?'

I nodded.

'And only a short way within sight and sound of camp at all times. Right?'

I nodded again.

'*Right.*' He picked up the .375, glanced at Greg and said: 'Let's go, as they say on the telly. Back about two, or just after, Emma.'

Before falling asleep the previous night I had decided to write to my mother. Apart from a cable sent from Chundi to tell her of my safe arrival, I had not so far written a single line home; partly because there had been little to say, so far, I suppose, but mainly because I had still felt anger towards her on my father's behalf.

But now, I was beginning to have second thoughts. Within minutes of Greg's Land-Rover, with Nick at the wheel, leaving the camp I had discovered myself fighting down an apprehension that could all too easily have grown to a state of panic. Around me there was nothing but beauty, silence and peace. And yet, not too far away, without so much as a picket fence between us, there wandered all the wild life for which the continent of Africa was famous. It was a sobering, not to say a frightening, thought.

And so, somehow, sitting on my canvas chair with my writing pad on my knee, I found myself feeling closer to my mother, despite the thousands of miles that lay between us, than I had ever done; also admitting to myself, for the first time, that in leaving my father and wiping him out of her memory (and mine) she might — just might — have had something of a case.

I thought of Kelly and the condition he was in. Yet he, presumably, was the fitter, if one could call it that, of the two. In what state, then, might I expect to find my father? Could he, even, monstrous as the idea might be to me, actually be a patient at the Leprosarium? And if so, would I be allowed to see him?

For this I was determined to do. Somewhere locked away inside me there was still the deep conviction that marriage ought to be for keeps. I also knew that, despite my built-in inferiority complex regarding my Amazonian appearance, opportunities for marriage had occurred more than once during the past decade, had I cared enough to foster them; my sex *did* make a great deal of the running when it came to marriage proposals, whether we cared to admit it or not.

But I had always drawn back, for one

reason or another, after the third or fourth dinner engagement or weekend drive into the country. Perhaps I had always been just that little more expectant than my daintier counter-parts of being dropped, so had hastened to do the dropping myself. But I knew, deep inside me, that there was more to it than that.

For one thing, my heart hankered after none of my lost opportunities, simply because I had never been really in love. For, surely, if I had, I would have known it, and hung on for dear life?

Now that I faced the matter squarely I had to admit that my mother's deeply happy marriage with Allan had been my criterion, however I had tried to hide the fact from myself. They were so completely devoted, and so absolutely in accord, that not even I could deny it. But where did that leave my poor father, who had the prior claim? And so I *had* to find him, to meet and talk with him, to hear his side of the story, before it was too late; if only for my own peace of mind.

It was at this point in my reflections that it occurred to me to wonder whether in this determination there might lie some likeness between us; that my mad, impulsive flight into the wilds of Africa may be said to resemble my father's obsessive search for his precious diamonds. He had not, from what I had gathered so far, found the end of his own particular rainbow. Would I find mine?

I had still written little more than a page of my letter when I first became aware that the sunlight across the camp was growing dimmer; brightening again from time to time, but becoming more and more frequently obscured by a bank of cloud that I had not seen rising at my back.

By the time Thomas called me to a lunch of cold ham — probably one of the fringe benefits of Nick's deep-freezing facilities — and baked beans, the sky had become quite overcast, except in the west, and the air was noticeably cooler. I asked if it would rain.

He sniffed. 'Can Madam not smell? It has rained already. Over there.' He was quite right, too. I could smell it; a faintly acrid and quite delicious scent in the nostrils. 'It may come here. It may not;' was as far as he was prepared to go.

I had eaten lunch and was debating whether to finish my mother's letter, take a nap in my tent, or ask Amos to accompany me on a short walk, when he came hurrying towards me.

'Madam come,' he said. 'This man is awake. He says he must go.'

'Go? Go where? And what for? This is stupid, Amos. He is supposed to wait to see me.'

'He says no, Madam. He says he comes to know whether Boss Locke takes his message to the policeman in Chundi, and if he has found you. Not to see you.'

'Policeman? Oh, you mean Mr

Driscoll. The solicitor.'

'Yes, Madam.' He sounded impatient. 'Is man like police.' He frowned at my stupidity. 'Goes to court — police court. Like policeman.'

'Oh; yes.'

'Madam will come.' He turned away decisively and I rose to follow him, my feet dragging along reluctantly in his wake so that he turned again in irritation to wait for me.

'Does he — has he — ?' No, I could scarcely ask if he had washed, or if he still smelt so fiercely. 'Is he better?'

'I do not know, Madam. He stands — so.' Amos gave a graphic demonstration of a man swaying slightly on his feet, hooding his eyes with heavy eyelids and squinting at me from beneath them.

'But I don't understand. How could he still be drunk?' Unless, of course, I thought wryly, there was a bottle concealed somewhere among the tattered clothing. Wasn't it said that alcoholics, like drug addicts, became very cunning concerning their source of supply? He had wakened, and started immediately to indulge his craving —

'*Madam.*'

'All right. I'm coming.'

We were halfway between my tent and the straw rondavel which housed Kelly when he appeared in the door-way, and I saw him on his feet, and in daylight, for the first time.

He was probably not more than two or three inches shorter than Nick, had he stood upright. It was obvious, however, that he remained on his feet at all only by a superhuman effort. His shoulders sagged so that his back was bent, and his long arms hung, loose and simian-like, against his sides. His eyes, a bright, light blue, were clouded as though still battling with sleep — or stupor — and the resemblance between the hooded, heavy lids and Amos's mimicry struck me at once. He was as drunk, I realised sadly, as he had ever been.

But then, as his eyes met mine, the

cloudiness lifted for a moment and they blazed with panic, or fright, so that I wondered whether my father, in view of Kelly's pitiful condition, had warned him not to be seen by me.

But that, of course, was nonsense. My father did not know I was here. Kelly had not known I was expected until he arrived at the camp. Then I recalled Greg Tarrant's words about the bush telegraph. Even so, Kelly had been in the camp all night, in a drunken sleep.

He turned as though to run, and as I stepped forward I saw the broken boot flap open, and the poor torn toe began to bleed again. In a moment all disgust vanished, and only intense pity remained.

'Wait. Oh, wait,' I said, moving towards him. But when I was still a few paces away he put up a hand, palm towards me, and I could see the long, grimed fingers trembling as he tried to hold them upright.

'No more,' he said. 'No nearer.' The words came slowly and very deliberately from his lips. There was a precision about his diction that may have been due to the intense effort he must have been making to speak clearly. 'It is not fitting — ' There was no slurring of the 's', however.

I could feel my eyes swimming with tears, and brushed at them impatiently. 'Let me at least find you some shoes,' I begged. 'And your foot needs bathing — '

'You are Emma Callow?'

'Yes, yes. Please wait — come over to my tent. Mr Locke has a medicine chest and I can — '

'Like a goddess. So beautiful, and tall, and straight. I — he said you would be tall, like your grandmother, Diana Callow; that you would be a Diana, too. He wanted you to be called Diana. He said you were an — elegant child. Don't cry.'

'Mr Kelly — '

'No. *No*. No nearer. I forbid you, do you hear?'

'But I must — oh, *please*.' I moved forward again, and he took a wavering backward step. 'Due to circum-stances entirely — beyond my control I am not — not able — You will tell Mr Locke — ' He took a deep breath and began again, with so obviously great an effort that the tears now streamed unheedingly down my cheeks. This, I thought, is heroism. I don't care a damn if he *is* an alcoholic; he's still a gentleman, and a courageous one at that.

'He will not hunt much after two o'clock.' He raised his bearded face to look at the sky. 'And the rains will send him back to Chundi within forty-eight hours. Ask him to come,' he waved a hand behind him, ' — he will find a track, and a ron-rond-avel — '

He took another backward step, then, to my astonishment, he smiled, so that I could see the still-white teeth through the matted beard. 'I am glad,' he said simply, 'glad and proud to have seen you.' Then he turned and began to run, with a shambling, almost crablike gait, across the ridge and down the slope into the bush. He was out of sight almost at once.

Amos had not moved. He stood now, regarding my tear-streaked face uncertainly.

'Say my name, Amos,' I said. 'Do you know my name?'

He nodded, puzzled.

'Say it, then.'

'Madam — '

'No, my name. Emma Callow. Say it.'

'Emma — Cello-i.'

'Yes. That's what I thought.'

'Must I go to find him?'

'No. Bring me the rifle from my tent. Quickly, Amos.'

He seemed a long time, but perhaps it was merely that I travelled a long way, in my thoughts, while I waited. The almost universal African habit of sounding an 'a' more like an 'e', and of adding an 'ey' suffix to almost every word that ended with a consonant seemed suddenly uncannily familiar. And over the years, as he sank deeper into an alcoholic haze of bitter disappointment and despair, he had let it be.

Yet Nick, I thought, with a sudden flash of comprehension, had known; had guessed, last night, when he stood looking down at him. And when he caught my eye, and saw the disgust in my face he had turned away, and left me in merciful ignorance.

Because nothing, probably, had ever disgusted Nick in his life. He was that rare being, a man of complete and unquestioning compassion towards all living creatures. Even Emma Callow.

I heard Amos hurrying towards me, and turned. 'Don't carry it like that,' I called, running to intercept him. 'Never carry a rifle with the barrel pointing — here, give it to me.'

'Is loaded, Madam.' He grinned and added: 'And one up the spout.'

I checked the safety catch, nodded, and glanced at my watch. 'It's well after one already, but I can't wait, I'm afraid. When the Land-Rover gets back tell Boss Locke that I've gone after Kelly.' I pointed. 'Down there. I'm taking the rifle for safety. Just in case — but it's open ground most of the way.'

'Madam must not go.'

'Why not? My — *he's* gone, and he must know whether it's safe. He can't even run fast enough — '

Amos showed his teeth in a grin. 'If buffalo come, nobody can run fast enough, Madam. Boss say you stay here — '

'No. There's no time, Amos. I must go after him. He might be — be dying. It's not far. It can't be or he'd never make it. They'll be back in just over half-an-hour. Tell them where I've gone, and why, and please ask Boss Locke to come after me.' I turned away from the adamant black face and ran across the rising ground.

From the ridge beyond which Kelly had disappeared it was possible to see quite a distance, I found. But the ground undulated so that there were dips and hollows of golden scrub, and deep, dry gullies — which I suspected would be awash when the rains began

— spread downwards like spider's legs towards the river.

I check the safety-catch again, then began to run down the slope. But not too fast. He might, I feared, have collapsed and fallen somewhere along the way, and I did not want to miss him. I was sure, in my mind, that he was dying, and I suppose this was my only excuse for what must have seemed to Amos — or to anyone else, for that matter — an act of utter madness.

I did not know where I was, or where I was going. Wild game were being hunted within a mere ten-mile radius of the camp, the safety of which I had left behind me. Only the day before, the mere glimpse of an elephant in the undergrowth, seen from the comparative safety of Nick's Land-Rover, had terrified me. I was indeed, as he had said, a city girl, and no heroine.

But if Kelly were dying, or as weak as he seemed to be — from lack of food, if nothing else — I still reasoned that he could not, even by summoning every ounce of reserve he had, travel either far, or fast. It could therefore be only a matter of minutes before I found him, or his place of shelter.

In the event I saw only a herd of some species of antelope, moving as one, with great speed, across a small open plain beyond the river, and a cluster of baboons who gibbered and chattered at my approach. I slowed to a walk as I passed, feeling instinctively that to appear afraid might be danger-ous; sure enough, they lost interest and swung away into the bush almost before I had gone by.

I was looking for a roof of some kind, yet when I searched among the scrub with my eyes I nearly missed it; the grey-brown of the thatch was an almost perfect camouflage amid the spindly tree trunks that surrounded it.

This *had* to be it. As I stumbled into the coarse, stalky undergrowth towards it I realised with surprise that it was a more permanent building than I had expected. It was a rondavel, but a larger one than I had so far seen, with plastered walls that had once been greenwashed, and upon which small curling chips of paint still remained.

A path of sorts led, not only up to it, but beyond, widening and curving out of sight among the trees. There was only one door, and this stood slightly ajar. As I reached it I saw that the bottom panels were ragged where termites had eaten them away, and small tunnels of packed sand traced erratic routes upwards and across the woodwork where the destructive white ant still foraged.

For the first time, I was afraid. Afraid to push the door open, afraid even to knock. Suppose there were snakes (or something larger) behind the door of this deserted hovel? Suppose some leper, refusing the Mission's help, were hidden here; even worse, that he might come to the door, with scabrous face, upon my knock?

But might that not be what was wrong with Kelly? Why he had found solace in drink and why he had warned me to come no closer? I remembered, with shame, Nick's words concerning the illness, and stooping, picked up a small rock from the path and beat upon the door with a force that swung it open upon protesting hinges so that I could see into the dimness beyond.

Incredibly, there was furniture, of a kind. What had once been a table of reasonable quality stood in the centre of the granolithic floor; white ant was at work here too, however, and had forced up the flooring in places so that wide cracks gaped, exposing the loose, fine sand that marked their progress. One or two armchairs, threadbare now, stood about, and the bed under the one small window was not of the camping variety.

He lay upon it as he had lain at the camp, in a state of utter exhaustion, it seemed. This time both hands clasped his head, though loosely now as the fingers had relaxed in sleep.

I pushed the door wide for more

light. The sun had completely disappeared and heavy rain clouds hung low above my head so that it might have been dusk instead of early afternoon. Then I went across to him and felt for a pulse in the flaccid wrist, as I had seen Nick do, the night before.

I could not find it at first, and this alarmed me so that I leaned across him, seeking to feel his breath on my face while I held my own in sheer trepidation that I was, after all, too late.

Then I felt the faint beat — beat; very slow, but nevertheless there. He was alive.

I tried to wake him, the relief was so great. I shook his shoulder, gently at first, then harder. I put my mouth to his ear and whispered, then called. His head lolled and his brow, when I pushed back the matted hair, creased as though in agony.

He was very ill; that much was certain. I had found him, and now I would have to leave him in order to get help. It was so dark by this time that I had actually to wait until I was outside on the path again to see the time; a quarter to two.

If I hurried back I should catch the men arriving back at the camp; if not, they would soon appear. I tucked the Winchester under my arm, pulled the door as nearly shut as I could, and started back along the path.

Only this time, now that the urgency of the search was over, my heart was in my mouth. Every rustle was a snake, every tree trunk an elephant's, every patch of dry, amber grass a lion, waiting to spring. I remember praying that the baboons would be gone because I would never have the courage now to pass them again, and the thudding of my heart in my ears became the thunder of hooves somewhere ahead —

And surely I had not come so far? All the gullies looked alike, and I could not see the river at all. I turned to look behind me, seeking my bearings from the hill in the distance and willing my heart not to thump so loudly.

There was the ridge — or a ridge — in front of me. If I climbed along and up this nearest gully it would bring me to the top, and at least I would get a better view. Surely from there the camp would be at least in sight even if I had strayed a little off course.

As my feet began to slither on the rough stones of the dry river bed, I noticed for the first time what my ears had been unconsciously hearing for the last half-hour or so; the dull rumble of thunder, intermittent and still fairly distant, but getting steadily closer.

Absurdly, the moment I became aware of it I grew more frightened still, in case the noise closed my ears to sounds more dangerous and close at hand. Also, if I *had* lost my direction, I wanted desperately to be able to hear the Land-Rover's approach. I could not remember being more terrified since, as a small girl, I had feared myself alone at night in a deserted house.

There was nothing to do but to go on. All the same, I wished my heart would stop its thudding. What with that, the murky gloom — almost a twilight now — and the rumbling thunder —

I stopped again, listening. Thud, thud, thud. Louder and louder, and faster every second. It wasn't the blood pounding in my ears; it couldn't be. At that moment I heard the Land-Rover crashing through the scrub behind and beneath me.

I turned and looked below as the vehicle bounced and jolted on to the open ground I had just left. I could see Greg, rifle cocked as though waiting for Nick to draw to a halt for him to get something in his sights.

Something; but what? The thudding seemed to be behind me now, and as I stood, staring down, Nick flung himself out of the Land-Rover and began to yell. He was waving one arm in a frantic sideways gesture and his face was so contorted that he was almost unrecognisable.

Then I saw Greg's rifle pointing

beyond and above me, and turned.

The thud of the buffalo's hooves was almost deafening now, for all that he was still some distance away. But he was travelling fast, head down and slightly twisted, and his eyes glowed red as he charged towards me.

Afterwards, I realised that it must have been all over in seconds. At the time, it seemed an eternity.

Where, I wondered, did one shoot to kill a buffalo? I would have one chance, and one chance only. Even if the men were coming up behind me, rifles at the ready, they could never reach me before he did. They could shoot him, and would (suddenly I realised that this had been their ploy; they had headed him into the gully, away from the camp, and then driven round to cut him off); but not until he had charged me first.

I lifted the rifle and hugged the butt against my shoulder. One in the breech, Amos had said. Pray God he was right. I needed that bullet, now, because if he came much closer it would be too late to get him in my sights.

Between the eyes. I had no idea whether it was the right place or not, but it seemed as good as any, and at least it should stop him in his tracks until Greg or Nick could finish him.

He was coming straight towards me, which made it easier. His head was still lowered and there was a darkish stain behind the right horn; behind and below it, which I could see clearly. And then I had him, plumb centre.

Now, *now*. I braced myself against the kick (how hard *did* a .375 kick?), pulled the trigger, flicked the bolt back, and fired again.

I never even felt it. Not then at any rate. I think I staggered back a step or two on the sloping ground; apart from that I remained, standing and staring, while the terrifying, magnificent beast appeared to check, come on, then slide, fore hooves canting outwards under his great weight. And then he fell.

They reached me almost together, Greg moving beyond me at once to climb up to where the buffalo lay. He stood for a moment looking down at it, then raised his head and stared at me. The awe in his gaze was embarrassing, but heart-warming. 'Merciful Lord,' he whispered. 'Where in the name of heaven did you learn to shoot like that? Right between the eyes. She did it Nick. What a girl! Better get your samples, Nicholas my boy.'

Nick's hands were on my shoulders, and he was shaking me so that the rifle almost fell from my hands and clattered down on to the stones. Unbelievable as it seemed, sweet-tempered, imperturbable Nick was shouting at me, again and again: 'You blasted fool. You damn', *bloody* little idiot. You bl— '

I tried to swallow and couldn't, then I actually felt my eyeballs rolling upwards, and even Nick's furious bellowing died away.

9

We must have been very near the camp
after all, because when I came to again
we were actually entering the clearing,
and although it was the first faint of my
life, I could not believe that it had
lasted more than a few minutes. The
first sound I heard was Greg's voice,
raised in excitement as he drove. 'I *had*
hit him, Nick. I said I had, didn't I? But
he turned his head and the bullet must
have glanced off that bone behind the
ear because I saw a trace of blood
under the what d'you call it — '

'Wings of the atlas,' replied Nick
absently. I was lying in his arms as far
as the limited space would allow, and he
was engaged in laying a folded,
water-soaked handkerchief across my
brow. My head lay in the crook of his
arm, and the silver eyes were gazing
anxiously into mine as I opened them.

I gazed back at him, thinking of nothing but how much I loved him. I loved the way his brows came over his eyes like little roofs, and the wonderfully tender, almost agonised expression in his face as he looked down at me. I loved his gentle hands and sweet disposition. I would have given anything in the world at that moment to believe that the way he was looking down at me meant anything more than when he looked like that at kittens, sick dogs, women like Dora; or dying, tramp-like men.

My defences were down, I suppose, so that my face showed more than I had ever dreamed of letting it show in all my twenty-nine years. Whatever the reason, he gave me a brief, sweet smile, said: 'That's good. You're better,' and turned away. Then the Land-Rover shuddered to a halt and Greg flung open his door, climbed out and ran round to us to open ours.

He put out a hand. 'Let me help,' he said. The slightly awed expression still lingered in his eyes as he looked at me. 'Lift her — ' he began. Nick shook his head, climbed purposefully out, then reached in and picked me up as though I were a featherweight. I fought back a hysterical impulse to laugh.

'Nick. I'm all right. Let me down.'

'Be quiet.'

'But I'm quite — '

'Quiet, I said.' He began to walk suddenly towards my tent while Greg strode beside us, his arms laden with rifles. He was grinning at me. 'He carried you all the way down the gully to the Land-Rover,' he said, 'so I suppose he might as well finish the job.' Then he lifted a hand to the brim of his hat, saluting me, and walked on.

I think it was at that moment that I really came to myself. 'Nick. Oh, Nick, put me down. There's no time. My father — '

He stopped suddenly, looking down at me searchingly. Then he set me carefully on my feet, keeping an arm about my shoulders. 'Your father? What about him?'

'Kelly. He's my father. Isn't he? You knew. You knew last night when — '

'Guessed, perhaps. Yes, I guessed.' He waited, watching me intently.

'He ran away. I went to find him because he was so ill. I *had* to. I wouldn't have left the camp after what you'd said for any other reason. But I had to find him again before he — *is* he dying, Nick?'

'I think he might be.' His voice was very gentle. 'I think he very well might be, Emma.'

I felt my face begin to crumple; my controlled, self-contained face that I had worn like a mask for so many years. I was too late, after all. Too late to *know* him, now. Just as I was already too late in beginning to understand my mother's point of view, all those years ago, for it to matter to either of us any more. We were stuck, now, in a relationship of half-hostility that it was almost certainly far too late for me to do anything to improve.

And Nick; I was *far* too late for Nick. The Nicks of this world do not look for girls with faces as remote and cool as enamel, who wear even a pair of denims — what had he said? — as though they were about to walk on to a film set. I was as wrong for him in every way as a girl could be, and at twenty-nine it was far too late to change. Too late, now, to fall in love; and too late now for me to help myself.

I began to sob; terrible, deep, tearing sobs that shamed me so that I buried my face in my hands. I could not remember, ever, having wept like this before. ('You're too *tall* to cry, Emma.') Every nerve, every muscle in my body seemed to be keening, and I could not control the low, moaning sound that came between each wracking sob. I was crying like a child, not an adult; and I could not stop.

It did not seem to matter to Nick, however. He did not appear to find anything reprehensible in the spectacle of an over-tall, self-contained gawk of a woman weeping against his shoulder as uncontrollably as if she were making up for all the unshed tears; all the griefs and resentments, large and small, from time immemorial, in one fell swoop.

He did not tell me to pull myself together. He did not not even murmur comforting nothings. There was no: 'Now come along, Emma. Don't cry like this.' Or: 'There, there.' He did not, in fact, say anything at all. He just held me closely against him while his shirt got wetter and wetter from my tears, his broad shoulder as solid and immovable as a rock against my head. Never in my whole life could I remember having had a shoulder to cry on before. Never, except in secret, had I wept so unrestrainedly; not even as a child. Especially not as a child.

I moved at last to grope for a handkerchief. I tried to speak while he took it from me and mopped my face. 'We must — '

'In a minute, Emma. I don't think it's going to make much difference either way. When you're ready we'll take the Land-Rover and go round the way Greg and I went after the buffalo, then we can pick him up and bring him here.'

'My face.' I touched my puffy, swollen eyelids and blotched cheeks with my fingers. I felt as though I had been briefly and terribly ill, and was just coming out of it; a kind of relaxed weakness pervaded my whole body.

'It's beautiful. *You're* beautiful. Surely you know that, Emma?' I was staring at him wonderingly. He began to laugh. 'I do believe you *don't* know it!' He put his hands on my face, running his fingers lightly over my cheek bones and down towards my chin.

'Such bones. And these little hollows, here. You have nothing to worry about. You're a very brave and beautiful girl, Emma. The bravest and most beautiful girl I've ever known.'

His face was very close to mine. He slid his hands down on to my shoulders, and then somehow my arms were about his neck and he was kissing me; a long, hard kiss that actually hurt, because I was kissing him back so fiercely. And even while we stood, locked in each other's arms, something inside me was saying: Make the most of it, Emma. This will never happen again. You aren't at all his kind of girl, remember. He's simply comforting you; he saw your heart in your eyes when you looked up at him in the Land-Rover, and he's being kind to a love-sick female who's a bit distraught.

It had to end, of course. And I had to be the one to end it; to move away from him first. He stood for a moment looking down at me, his eyes tender, but with a faint twinkle lurking in their depths. Then his manner changed completely.

'Better get some blankets,' he said. 'It'll be chilly when this storm breaks.' He turned towards our tents and I hurried along beside him.

'D'you think it will? It seems to have

been rumbling around for hours.'

He looked up at the blue-black clouds massing over our heads. 'Oh, I think so.' He pointed eastwards. 'It's coming from the right direction. There's a tarpaulin in the Land-Rover. We have to try and keep him dry. I'll get Thomas to lay some blankets down in the back. Go and collect my rifle from Greg, just in case.'

We reached the rondavel in no time at all, it seemed. Apart from the group of Minzandan field staff from the camp who crouched over the carcass of the buffalo, knives at the ready, we saw nobody.

'Good eating there,' said Nick, in reply to my questioning glance. 'They won't waste an ounce of that fellow. They'll cut him into moveable hunks and load him on to their Land-Rover, and take the lot into camp.' He braked as he spoke, then turned and gave me a speculative look.

'You certainly had me fooled, back there. I couldn't see any possible way out of it. If we'd fired, we'd almost certainly have hit you, and I — we couldn't possibly get past you in time. Dear God, I thought you'd had it.'

It was his first allusion to my shooting exploit, and I stared down demurely at my hands as they lay in my lap, trying to force down the triumphant feeling that, at least once in our acquaintanceship, I had caught him completely off balance.

'Sorry about the language,' he said at last, awkwardly. 'If you heard it, that is. I've been hoping you didn't.' He paused as though waiting for an answer, but I did not reply. He must, however, have observed my faint smile.

'Like Greg,' he said at last, 'I'm all agog to know where you learned to shoot like that.' He began to ease the Land-Rover gently forward again.

'Simple, really. It's always been Allan's — my step-father's — thing. He's been shooting at Bisley for years. Then Brian — my brother — got interested. He's really very good.

'Then one day — oh, a couple of years ago now — I was home for the weekend and they took me along to the Rifle Club. Allan showed me how to hold the rifle — a .303 — and let me have a go. I nearly hit the bull's eye.' I laughed. 'Nearly broke my collar bone too.

'They didn't believe it, of course. Said it was just a fluke — beginner's luck. I felt sort of exhilarated, though, and insisted on trying again.' I sat for a moment in amused recollection of Brian's schoolboy chagrin and Allan's quite genuine appreciation.

'Allan said I must have a natural eye, or something, and began to coach me seriously. Before long I was better than Brian, and — according to Allan — as good as he was any day.

'Brian's a nice boy, and a good sport really. But he's never really forgiven me for being a better shot than he is. It's become his Achilles heel, I think; he can't accept that a female can possibly be better than a male in what is usually regarded as a male preserve. Allan asked me to go along with them the very weekend — ' I hesitated, and then went on, 'the last time I was home. You could see the relief on Brian's face when I refused.' I looked up to find him smiling as he edged the Land-Rover along the rutted track.

'But he's not nineteen yet. And he *can* laugh at himself about it, so he's all right, really.'

Nick slowed as we reached the bush beyond the clearing, while I found my bearings, and searched with my eyes for the thatched roof among the trees.

'There. There, look, where the track widens.'

'H'm. Looks as though someone had cut a road, or a driveway, at some time.' He drove forward again, carefully now, backing the vehicle against the jagged door. He helped me down, then stood for a moment, hands in pockets, staring along the track to where the bend hid it from sight.

'Some old ruin or other along there, I

expect. An old farm, or a disused mine even, perhaps.' He shrugged and laid the flat of his hand against the door, pushing it gently but firmly open against the same protesting creak that I had raised with the blow from my stone.

It was very dark indeed now inside the desolate, circular room. 'There's a torch in the back, Emma. Fetch it, will you?' Without waiting he disappeared from view, stooping beneath the lintel as though from long-ingrained habit.

When I reached him, torch in hand, he was leaning over my father, almost mouth-to-mouth, as I had seen him do at the camp. He took the torch from me and switched it on, lifting one of the closed eyelids and shining the light directly into it while I stood beside him, looking down at all that was left of Andrew Grant Callow.

'He's — he's so thin,' I said at last. 'He can't have been eating at all, Nick.'

'No. But then, he wouldn't.' Nick seemed completely preoccupied as he unfastened the pitiful strands of shoelace that held the tattered jacket together and drew it back to reveal the skeleon-like torso. I moved towards my father and lifted one of his hands, holding it between my own. It was odd, the way in which the grime between the fingers and under the long, curling nails had ceased to matter. All I knew at that moment was the terrible aching knot in my throat at the knowledge that this poor derelict should be my own father, and that I had not known it soon enough to have been able to do anything, however small, to help him.

'Is he — is he still alive, Nick?' Now, I could feel no pulse at all.

'Yes.' Suddenly, Nick leant over him, grasped his shoulders firmly, and began to shake him. 'Come on, Andrew. Andrew, d'you hear me?' He put his mouth against his ear, and shouted, as he had shouted at me. 'Kelly! Callow! Andrew! Hoy!'

For a second I imagined I saw an eyelid flicker faintly, then Nick laid him down again.

'Don't — don't hurt him,' I whispered.

Nick gave a short laugh. 'I'd willingly hurt him if I thought it would bring him round.'

'Bring him round?' But if he's sick as well as drunk — '

Nick straightened and looked at me for the first time since I had entered the hut, his jutting brows low over his eyes. 'Drunk?' he said. He shook his head slowly.

'Well — isn't he?' His eyes held mine while I stammered: 'But I thought — didn't Greg — oh, *everybody* say — ?' My voice trailed away, while he stared at me, then I added haltingly: 'I don't understand anything at all. Everybody thought he was drunk. I did myself. So did you.'

He looked at my father, and back at me. 'But not for long. You know,' he said gently, 'we nearly always see what we expect to see — haven't you noticed? When your father first appeared at the camp — a white derelict, it would seem, any Minzandan would assume he was an alcoholic. They've seen enough of 'em; the types who get bushed from solitude and go to pieces. When I saw him it was dark — I met him in the shadows because he wouldn't come any closer to the fire — and he was swaying on his feet, even then.'

'Yes. That's what I mean. Then last night — '

'Last night he was already out on his feet when we saw him. Even so — '

'You didn't think he was drunk, last night?'

'No. No, I didn't.' He waved a hand at the room. 'See any empty bottles, Emma?'

'No.' And indeed there were none.

'I smelt his breath in the camp last night. Anybody as stoned as he seemed to be would have reeked of it. That was when I began to wonder — '

'Wonder what? Whether he was my father?'

'Oh, that. No. I think I guessed that when he gave me the cheque, but there seemed no point in saying so to anyone at that time. If he wanted to make a secret of it he had his reasons, no doubt. In any case, it was entirely his own affair.' He gave me his slow, sweet smile. 'And how was I to know what his daughter would be like? How was I to know she'd have the guts and staying power to come out here to find him, and work it out for herself when she did?'

He put out a hand and took mine.

'But — what *is* it then, Nick? Can you tell?'

'I — *think* so. As I said, we see what we expect to see. A man with a teetotaller for a wife, who comes home to find her roaring drunk, will never think of that. He'll be sure she's ill, to begin with at any rate; never that she's tight. Why should he, when it's never happened before? And it applies the other way round, as with your father.

'There are quite a few types of illness, you know, that can give the impression of drunkenness; diabetes is one. But in this country, and in this particular area, only one comes to mind that produces exactly the symptoms we've seen in your father.' He paused, and I think it was at that moment that the uncharacteristic deviousness of this conversation got through to me. Quite simply, he didn't want to tell me what that illness was.

Poor Nick, I thought. You've really been lumbered with us; my father and me. And none of it has anything whatsoever to do with you. That it was the first time this cold, hard fact had really occurred to me made me hot with shame. Those people who are quite incapable of passing by on the other side are a very rare breed indeed, and it struck me then, as we stood side by side in the shadows behind the bright beam of the torch, that the rest of the world were only too eager to exploit them for all we were worth. It was painfully explicit to me, in that rare moment of self-revelation, that that was precisely what I had been doing.

'Tell me, Nick. It's all right. Honestly. What is it, d'you think?'

'He has sleeping sickness. Trypanoso-miasis. I'm sure of it, now.'

'*Oh*.' I was back at school again, remembering the horrors of imagining one had a disease as a result of hearing about it in class. Leprosy had been my own particular demon; whenever scripture lessons brought it under discussion I would spend the rest of the day searching my hands and arms for tell-tale white blotches, and it would be days before the fear stopped haunting me. Sleeping sickness was another. I had never even heard of it until my form mistress, seeing me yawning my head off with boredom during class one morning, had remarked with asperity: 'Emma Callow appears to be suffering from sleeping sickness. Or am I boring you?'

I had wandered about all that day, stifling incipient yawns and feeling quite terrified, when at last I laid my head on my pillow, of falling asleep in case I might never wake again.

'Can — can it be cured?'

'Oh, yes. Well, it can if it's caught in time.' He bent over my father again and began patiently looping the laces through the holes in his jacket, frowning fiercely as though in deep concentration.

But I knew it wasn't that. He was waiting for my next question, and dreading it.

'How did he catch it?' I had to spare him a moment or two at least. 'From an — a — what is it? — a host animal?'

'No, no. Oh, Emma, there are many ways. Not that it's all that common — it isn't — but your father hasn't been living a normal sort of life for some time, I'd say. You see — '

'From a tsetse fly? What are they like?'

'A bit like — well, a horse fly. Not directly from a tsetse fly, no.' He was beginning to sound more like his old self; the earnestness I remembered when he talked about his work at

Blake's on the night of my arrival creeping back into his manner, and the now-familiar crease appeared between his brows.

'You remember the long shed, like a tobacco barn, that we passed on our way here from Chundi?'

'You mean the one where you said vehicles in transit have to go in to be sprayed? We didn't though, did we?'

'Because we were *entering* a tsetse area, not leaving one. On our way back we shall be directed to drive in at one end, have the whels sprayed, and then drive out through the other.

'Tsetse flies like the shade. The underside of a stationary car bumper is a favourite resting place. It's the parasite they leave behind that's so deadly, not the fly itself. Oh, and the trunks of trees. They rest on the shady sides of trees, so it could be that your father — ' He waved a hand towards the window, where splotches of battleship-grey sky glowered between the foliage beyond the hut. Then he sighed and added: 'Who knows, at this stage?'

'It's — a late stage, Nick, is it?'

'I'm afraid so. He knew when he came looking for me, I think, as Kelly. I asked him why Callow hadn't come himself, you remember? Was he dying or something?'

'And he said he might be. But — oh, Nick, why didn't he tell you, then? What I can't understand — '

'It's possible that he felt it was already too late for a cure. Or perhaps he didn't care enough to try.' Nick handed me the torch and, stooping low, lifted the limp form tenderly in his arms. The murky light from the window caught his face as he straightened, so that I could see him hesitating, trying to choose his words.

'It's not one hundred per cent curable, you see, even in the early stages; not by a long shot. Mortality rate's as high as twenty to twenty-five per cent, or so I believe. *He'd* know that, you know, living in the bush, *and* in a tsetse area, as long as he has.'

Didn't care, I thought. Didn't care enough even to try to live. I turned to follow Nick, then moved ahead of him to draw back the door to its widest point. 'Do you think he's suffered much? Is it — is there any pain?'

'It's the head, mainly. Blinding headaches, as a rule, with no relief during consciousness. And the lethargy of course, getting steadily worse all the time, so that everything — eating, bathing, even staying awake — becomes too much trouble.'

I remembered the way his fingers semed always to have been clutching his head, and the way he had stood, weaving slightly before me, at the camp. 'No nearer — '

'Nick. Why didn't he let me help him? Is it catching? Was he afraid I might — ?'

'No.' He pressed his back against the scrofulous door so that small tunnels of sand cracked slightly here and there and exploded in powder-like puffs against his shoulders and bare arms. His tone was a little impatient as he added:

'He's *dirty*, Emma. He'll have been conserving what energy he had during these past weeks for staying awake long enough to find out about you. He'd have none left to expend on keeping himself clean. Come on, now, the first spots are falling. We'll have a deluge any minute.'

I watched him lay my father gently on the spread blankets in the back of the Land-Rover, then turned to pull the door as shut as it would go.

It was the first time, I suppose, that it had stood so wide since I had found my father's poor dwelling. For this reason, perhaps, I had not previously glimpsed the oblong glint of white balanced against the wall on the corner of the sideboard. I ran across and peered at the writing on the envelope, then remembered the torch and switched it on. For me? A message from my father? A thrill of hope swept through me. It would not be much; but it would be something.

To Whom It May Concern, I read. Not then, exclusively for me.

'Emma. What are you doing? Let's — what's that you've got?'

'I don't know. I haven't opened it. I found it over there.' I pointed. 'Propped against the wall.' I stared at him, puzzled. 'But, Nick, he can't have written it since — '

'No. No, he can't. It's probably been there some time.' He raised his voice on the last few words as a rushing, roaring sound, gaining in volume, swept towards us from somewhere beyond the belt of trees. There was something frightening about it, and I think he saw my alarm.

'It's all right, The rain's come.' He took my hand and pulled me outside. 'Better be quick or we'll get marooned here, as like as not. We're on fairly low ground. Look.' He pointed towards the way we had come, and I gazed, fascinated, at a sight I had never seen before.

The clouds appeared to touch the ridge, they hung so low, and the rain was a solid sheet, drenching the yellow-brown earth so that it gleamed like gun-metal as the water began first to trickle, then to cascade down towards the river. As we watched, the sheet of rain moved towards us like a thick curtain, while we stood on bone-dry ground outside the hut.

Nick wrenched open the door of the Land-Rover, bundled me inside, and was climbing into his seat as the first enormous drops spattered the bonnet. He slammed the door shut, thrust a hand through his hair, and gave me a triumphant nod.

'Thank heaven for that.' He glanced behind at my father's unconscious form. 'At least we didn't get him wet. We'll need that tarpaulin, though, when we lift him out at the camp. Better get cracking.'

We ate in my tent that evening, flaps firmly secured against the storm; then returned, tarpaulin held above our heads, to the straw rondavel where my father lay, and from which he had fled that morning. Neither the short journey back to the camp nor the gentle handling that had been necessary to divest him of his clothing and gently sponge the emaciated body, had coaxed the slightest flicker of returning consciousness from him.

I bathed him myself, with Nick's help, but Nick refused to allow him to be over-disturbed.

'Look,' he said. 'A little grime won't hurt him, now. Let him be comfortable.'

'But he doesn't know — '

'No.' He lifted an eyelid again, and lowered it gently. 'All the same.'

'When will he come round again, Nick? I thought I'd stay here tonight. I'm afraid — suppose he woke and ran away again?'

'He won't.'

'But how can you be sure?' It was not only the fear that he might disappear into the storm, staggering and stumbling only to fall, perhaps face down, into the swirling waters of a gully, that had decided me not to leave him. I hoped, more than anything in the world, to be there when he opened his eyes. I wanted him to speak to me again; to admit to being my father. I wanted with all my heart to hold his hands in mine and tell him that it didn't matter; that nothing mattered but that we had found each other, and to let him see that I was not ashamed of him.

'Emma,' said Nick gently. 'You need your sleep. You've been up since the crack of dawn, and you've had a hell of a day. Besides, there's nothing you can do. He won't wake, I promise you. I — don't *think* he'll ever wake again. I think he's in a coma.'

'But how can you know?'

He dropped to his haunches beside me as I knelt by the bed. 'It's the way it goes, my dear.' Our eyes met and I found myself thinking: it's the first endearment he's used to me.

'It's nearly two months, by my reckoning, since he first turned up and gave me the message for Jerry Driscoll, to have you traced. He was already, even then, a sick man.' He lifted his shoulders and let them fall.

'Perhaps then, if only he'd told us; perhaps at that time we might have saved him; I simply don't know. But you have to remember that he's had no treatment during that time; that much is pretty obvious. If he'd only gone to the Mission they'd have helped. They have qualified doctors there.

'As it is,' he slid an arm about my shoulders and drew me towards him. 'You have to face it, Emma. Untreated, it's a disease that can only end its course in death, and it's a pretty short course at that.'

'How — how long?'

'Three months. Lethargy, loss of energy, then drowsiness and an overwhelming compulsion to sleep, leading to coma; and death. That's it. Your father is in a deep coma; I'm sure of it.' He rose, suddenly, adding almost angrily: 'Do you think I wouldn't have tried to get help, to get him even as far as the Mission, if I'd seen any sense in it, even through this?' He waved a hand at the din above our heads. 'We'd never make it; not a hope. I don't mind about being bogged down for the night out there; not for myself. But it's a hell of a way for a dying man to breathe his last. This way, at least, we're with him; there's light and a little comfort. To die in the dark, in the back of a Land-Rover, marooned in a storm miles from anywhere, there's no dignity in it at all.' The Scots accent was more marked than I had ever heard it.

I looked back at him dully. I must still have been hoping, then, because now I felt as though there were a leaden weight within me. It could only mean that hope had finally died. 'You couldn't drive anywhere in this, I know that. There isn't even a road to follow. And the Mission's — the Leprosarium's — across the river, anyway. Near Diamond Hill; I saw it.

Where's the nearest bridge?'

He flapped an arm. 'About twelve miles on along the road from Chundi. The river cuts across it.'

'And it's a dirt road.'

'Yes.' He was frowning down at my father's still face. 'And the Mission's well off the road;' he grinned bleakly. 'Off the map, just about. I'd never make it, and that wouldn't do him any good at all.' I realised suddenly that against all reason, against his own judgement, and his conviction that my father was beyond all help, he had actually been considering it for some time — for my sake.

'Oh, no, Nick. I didn't mean that.' I pushed myself to my feet in protest. 'We'll do as you said; get through to Chundi at first light tomorrow and report, then take him to the Mission. That's if the rain stops.'

'It'll stop; probably during the night. And you have no idea how quickly the ground hardens again. That's what soil erosion is all about. There's no top soil left in undulating country like this; it's all been washed away, into the river for the most part, long ago.' He was still frowning down at my father. I slid a hand absently into the pocket of my denims, encountered a wedge of paper, and pulled it out. It was the envelope.

10

It seemed incredible at first that I could possibly have forgotten it. But then, why not? In the rush of getting back to the camp before the storm reached its height, helping to make my father comfortable, and struggling, under Nick and Greg's watchful gaze, to eat, I had never given it a further thought. After all, the man who had written it would wake again, sometime (or so I had thought) and what use a mere letter from him, then? Besides, it was not even addressed to me.

I handed it to Nick, silently. 'Good Lord,' he murmured. 'I'd forgotten all about it.' He looked at me question-ingly and, when I nodded, slid a thumbnail beneath the flap. Then he put out an arm and drew me towards him, so that we could read it together in the light from the hanging Tilley.

It was not, strictly speaking, a letter at all. It was as though he had been endeavouring to keep a sort of diary, or a log, which had in the end proved too much of an effort. The date in the top right-hand corner read September 1st. There were three unnumbered sheets. The first began:

'It is being borne upon me that I am a sick man. I thought at first that it may be malaria — it would not be the first attack I have had — but the symptoms are wrong. I am sure, now, that I have contracted sleeping sickness. I do not know how far the disease has progressed, but I am sleeping for longer and longer periods so that I am losing count of the days, and the pain in my head is very bad. This is a symptom I did not know about, which is why I began by treating myself for fever instead of seeking help. I fear that it is now too late.

'I write this because it may be that at some future time someone will discover my remains and I have no desire to cause unnecessary trouble to anyone. My name is Andrew Grant Callow. I have contrived to set in motion certain machinery in an attempt to trace my only relative; my daughter, born Emma Jane Callow, one time of Fleetchurch, Sussex, England.

'I ask whoever may find this to hand it to Messrs Lowell and Driscoll, Solicitors, of Chundi. My assets in the Chundi Branch of Emerson's Bank should be sufficient to meet the costs of tracing my daughter and of providing her with a small legacy. Lowell and Driscoll have my will in their keeping.'

There was a further entry for September 2nd, but it was very short:

'Head very bad today. Must go up to the house while I am still mobile. Would like my daughter to have — '

The next date was September 9th.

'Difficult to concentrate. Doesn't matter. Only want to sleep. No wish to see my daughter. Too many years now. Should not like to see her ashamed. Borehole dry and can no longer reach the house to wash. Doesn't matter. She would not remember me at all, anyway. Wonder whether she is her mother's daughter, or mine? Was like her grandmother Callow as a child. Wonder if she remembers her birthday candles? Pretty rainbow colours. She loved pretty colours. Too strict. Too strict. Barbara always — Too tired.'

I tried to move away from Nick's restraining arm, but he held me firmly. The tears that blinded my eyes prevented me from reading further, and this he seemed to sense.

'September 15th's the next date. The writing's falling off, and it's getting pretty disjointed, Emma. Let me read it to you.

''She had a little doll she liked, yet she left it behind. I wonder why? I gave it to her, so perhaps Barbara — I must not say harsh things about Barbara. She hated Africa; so much that in the end I believe she even grew to hate me. It was right to take the child away. I see that now. Only hope Barbara loves her enough; Emma is a Callow, too, like me. I hope —

"'And the candles. But she got the better of her mother there, in her own small way. Indomitable child. No tears, no fuss. Too self-contained for such a baby. Yet I used to take her on my knee and she liked it well enough. Wonder if she ever found another knee to sit on? Too proud, perhaps. Her only defence I suspect —

"'I am rambling, and there is something I wish to say. Important, I think. Cannot remember now. It will come. Must find out which camp Locke visits this tour, and see him if possible. Have come to rondavel to be nearer.'"

Nick frowned. He was, I noticed, keeping his voice deliberately matter-of-fact as he read, raising it above the din of the thunder and rain so that I could hear.

'He didn't find me, though,' he said. 'Probably couldn't make it. I was at Impala in September, I think.'

'Impala,' I repeated.

249

He glanced at me, puzzled. 'Yes, Impala.' Then he smiled. 'Nice word, isn't it?' I nodded.

'Beautiful, gazelle-like creatures.' He flipped another page. 'Quite a man, this father of yours. Imagine struggling with something like this in his condition. Concentration must have been sheer hell.'

'I wonder why?' I brushed at my wet cheeks with my hand. Oddly, I felt completely unselfconscious about my tears; they were a mere irritation in that they prevented me from reading for myself. As for Nick, it was as though, to him, weeping was as natural as breathing in the circumstances, and he completely ignored them.

'Oh, Emma, don't you know? Can't you see? For Whom It May Concern, indeed. He meant this for *you*. A man who knows he hasn't got long to go, with only one person of his flesh and blood in the world, and that one thousands of miles away, as far as he knows.

'It's a terrible thing to die alone, Emma. Entirely alone. He *had* to talk to someone, if only on paper. Who better than you?'

'If only he'd gone to the Mission! Or let you take him to Chundi with you. Anything but this — '

'You know, he was probably right in believing it was too late. And *he* was proud, Emma. That's probably where you've got it from. He couldn't bear to be seen in his condition, and identified as Andrew Callow. He must have retreated further and further into himself over the years; he'd know he had nothing to offer you. That's almost certainly why he never tried to find you before. He'd genuinely think you were better off without him.'

'But — how did he live, Nick? He'd stopped prospecting, yet he had money in Chundi.'

'Well, it wouldn't do him much good here. Apart from the odd African store run by the farmers for their workers, where would he buy anything? He was a hunter once, remember. He'd be a marvellous shot, you know. They all are; have to be. Wouldn't last long if they weren't.' He grinned faintly at me, and squeezed my shoulder. 'Must be another thing his daughter inherited; the hunter's true eye. If it interests you to know it, you're streets ahead of me with a rifle in your hands, and your young brother has my entire sympathy. He'd live off the land, perhaps. Until — this happened to him.'

'Was there a gun in the hut? I didn't see — '

'No. Nor did I. But then, we weren't looking, were we?'

'Go on, Nick. There's more, isn't there?'

'Yes.' He had been waiting, then, until he felt I could take it. Oh, Nick, I thought. Dear, darling, compassionate Nick. If only I could say it aloud, instead of only to myself.

'H'm. Quite a long gap. Getting longer every time. October 2nd. Very short, this.

252

''She liked the rainbows. Thought they came down inside the house. Barbara told her you can never find the end of a rainbow — I showed her you could. Walked her to where the strands of colour struck the tops of the trees and slanted on to the ground. Didn't want to look for pot of gold; only rainbow end. Not an avaricious child, thank God. I would have liked — liked to — would have — ''

Nick looked at me. 'Funny thing, that,' he said. The weather here comes across from the south-east, mostly. Local showers by the yard from now on through the season. From the ridge you can stand and see them — four, five, six local storms, with each rain cloud touching the ground, as we saw it last night. And towards the west, over Diamond Hill, if it's clear, you'll see rainbows galore, one after the other, arching over the hill, and the Mission, and coming down to earth this side of the river, round about where we found your father. If it's clear enough tomorrow we may see one.'

'Is — is there any more? He lost himself, about there, didn't he, Nick? I wonder what it was he would have liked?' My throat was aching. 'If only I could have given it to him.'

'I think you did. I think it was to see you before he died. And remember, Emma, he got his wish. What did he say — can you remember?'

I would never forget. But I could not tell even Nick; or not all of it.

'"I am glad and proud to have seen you."'

'He said that?'

'He said that.'

'I'm so glad. I'm so *damn*' glad, darling. There's not much more.' He frowned down at the last sprawling sentences in the yellow light of the Tilley. He seemed completely unaware of what he had just called me.

'October 25th. But that's only a few days ago.' Nick shot an incredulous glance at my father. 'It doesn't seem possible.'

'He spoke to me this morning. It was a battle for him, but he did it.'

'Fantastic. This is difficult, Emma. I'll have to try to decipher it bit by bit; it's barely legible.

''She would have — no — *should* have a small something, but I have found only one in all these — (years, I think it is). That was the night — we never saw again — (I think he means he never saw you again) — I thought there would be more, but never — all the years I have searched —

''Emma's — (something) — hidden. I have put if she should ever come to find me she will know where — nobody else in the world would dream — If she does not — doesn't matter. Nobody else.''

'That's all there is, Emma. I'm not sure about that last bit. Does it mean anything to you?'

I shook my head. 'No. But as he says, it doesn't matter. It doesn't matter at all. Only that he wrote to — for me; that's all that matters.'

The rain began to slacken at about four o'clock that morning. With its easing the thunder died away, but now a new sound was audible; the sound of water rushing wildly from the high ground and pouring in torrents down the gullies — the bone-dry gullies of little more than twelve hours ago — towards the river.

By five the rain had stopped entirely, and the sound of rushing water had lessened considerably. My father still breathed, locked in his private, unconscious world. Nick had dressed him in a spotless bush jacket of his own, and wound a blanket around the emaciated lower limbs. I had begged a pair of sharp scissors from Nick's 'bag of tricks' and trimmed the beard and flowing hair. He looked peaceful, dignified and distinguished, like some sleeping archaeologist, or erudite don. Nick and I looked at each other, and smiled.

'A handsome man, your father,' he said. He held out a hand towards me.

'Come and see outside.' He led me out of the hut and on to the sodden ground.

It was still dark, and there was no moon, but I was astonished by the amount of light cast by the stars that studded the velvety, cloudless sky.

'All gone,' said Nick. 'Another hour and we'll be on our way to the Mission, I hope.'

'There's still an awful lot of water, though. D'you think — ?'

'All drained away, by then. Oh, the road'll be a bit treacly, but not so much as you'd think. Then when the sun comes up you'll see the steam begin to rise. Did you take your anti-malaria pill, girl?'

'Yes. Will it come back, the storm?'

He laughed. 'Which one? We've had about six hanging around us all night. That's why the thunder's so non-stop in these here parts at this time of year.'

'And the lightning.' I shuddered. 'I never did like lightning, even in England, but this — !'

'Were you frightened, then? I didn't realise. I'm sorry.'

'No. No, I don't think I *was* actually frightened. Too much else to think about, I suppose. Look, Nick. Is it growing light, over there?'

But even with the light of the dawn to help us, I marvelled at Nick's skill in manoeuvring the inimitable Land-Rover over such appalling terrain. For the first time, I saw for myself what experts meant when they talked of soil erosion. When we had arrived at the camp a mere two days I ago I had thought the going rough; now I could have laughed at my abysmal ignorance.

I sat in the back with my father, his head pillowed upon a cushion in my lap to spare him from the worst of the bumps. Nick drove very slowly indeed, but even without my father to worry about I doubt if we could have travelled faster. Sometimes, where the rush of water had scored deep ruts in the track, Nick was forced to abandon it and jolt through the bush, negotiating a path between gnarled tree roots that stood, in places, a foot or more above the ground. Again and again we had to slow almost to a halt, easing first the front, then the rear wheel over bumps and hollows that no ordinary vehicle could have attempted.

By the time we reached the main road, however, the sun was well up, and he shot a quick glance at me over his shoulder. 'Drying out nicely,' he said. 'And at least there'll be no dust. The treacly bits are the nasty ones.'

And indeed they were. Once, when we got caught in a patch and the Land-Rover slithered and slid, crab-wise, for what seemed an eternity before Nick regained control, my father's head slipped from my lap so that I barely caught it in time to prevent it from thudding against the metal coachwork, and I drew in my breath sharply. Nick must have heard me.

'Sorry.' Then, as though he knew: 'Wedge that blanket between you and the side — that's right. The terrain's changing — it's stony rather than sandy from now on down, so it should be fairly plain sailing.'

Nevertheless, I did not think I would ever forget that journey. When we left the road at the bridge — a narrow, ramshackle affair that clanked and heaved as we crept over it — we traversed a track almost as badly eroded as the one that led down from the Camp before striking a wider, firmer road where a stretch of open, gently-rising ground, like a small plain, brought the Mission buildings into view.

There was a church, in pink-washed stucco, the apex of its sloping roof carrying a plain wooden cross like a banner, and next to this what was evidently the priests' house. The long, plain building beside it could only have been a school, and as we approached I saw what appeared to be another house just behind it, also adorned with a cross.

'The Sisters' house,' said Nick in

reply to my question. 'They live there with a small sanatorium annexed to the house for any sick who may be too ill to be allowed back to their villages. There's a clinic beside the Fathers' house to treat the ones who are fit to come and go.'

'But who attends the school?'

'Villagers' children — or as many as they can take.'

'And the — Leprosarium?' Even as I asked I identified it. An archway some five hundred yards away from the main buildings, fashioned in wood and bearing the word LEPROSARIUM in roughly carved wooden characters, opened upon what appeared to be a largish village in its own right. There was no gate, so that I could see the long main street leading up to where small, whitewashed thatched houses began to line it on either side. Other streets branched off, and each house appeared to have its own tiny garden.

'It's pretty self-contained,' said Nick as he drew the Land-Rover to a halt outside the presbytery. 'They fend for themselves, you know, to a great extent. Two or three Sisters and a doctor treat them from a clinic inside the settlement. They grow most of their own food — things like that. And of course they're not allowed to come and go beyond the archway; at least, not until they're cured. But they have bags of freedom inside it.' He turned to me and smiled. 'And they do get cured; quite a lot of them. Believe me.'

He climbed down and came to assist me to alight. 'Lay him down — that's it. Then come with me. He'll be all right, and they'll have a stretcher they can lift him on to — '

'If they'll take him. How do we know they will?'

'They'll take him.' Nick placed a forefinger on the bell and pressed. 'That's what they're for, Emma. People like this don't say no.'

The door was opened by a bare-headed, greying man in a belted white habit that reached to his ankles. He saw

262

me first, and the bushy eyebrows lifted in surprise. Then his glance flickered to Nick, and he beamed at him.

'Why, Mr Locke. What a pleasure.' The accent was unmistakably Irish. 'Must be a year or more since we've seen you. Come in, come in. Can we help you?'

'You can indeed, Brother Crispin.'

The Brother glanced beyond us to the mud-spattered Land-Rover. 'A terrible journey you'll have had, I'm thinking, so it must be serious.'

He eyed me thoughtfully, his expression changing to one of sympthy and concern as Nick told him about my father, then hurried ahead of us to where he lay, still as a corpse, his head resting on the cushion so that his beard jutted slightly upwards, obscuring the features.

Brother Crispin leaned inside to take a wrist in his hand, could not quite reach, and swung himself up and into the vehicle. I saw his expression change as he gazed down into my father's face.

'Dear Lord,' he whispered, and there was real distress in his voice. 'It's Mr Kelly, God help us. Mr Kelly, come to this.' He knelt beside my father then, feeling for a pulse, and raising first one eyelid and then the other.

'We must get him inside.' He leapt effortlessly down, the habit notwithstanding, and hurried back to the house, where he seized a large handbell lying on a bench just inside the door and swung it in one resonant burst of sound.

Things seemed to happen pretty quickly after that. My father was lifted gently on to a stretcher and carried across to the Sisters' annexe, Nick and I following while Brother Crispin hurried ahead.

They laid him in a bed in a tiny cell-like room, although I had glimpsed a half-empty ward as we followed the stretcher-bearers along the corridor. The walls were white-painted, and a crucifix hung above the bed.

'Forgive me now while I fetch a

priest. Father O'Halloran was about just now. I'll see if I can find him.' He hurried out, and I heard him murmuring as he passed. 'Mr Kelly, now. Dear me.'

'A priest,' I said to Nick. 'Does he mean — will he be a doctor?'

'The Brother's a doctor himself. Or was, till he joined the Order. But there's a lay doctor here anyway; a chap called Wilde.'

'Oh? Then what does he want a priest for?'

'He doesn't think your father has much longer, Emma. Face it, darling; you must. He won't come round.'

I felt quite able to face it now, however. I knew I had already said the only goodbyes I would ever say in him. And somehow, lying here in this spotless bed, his gaunt face turned to the ceiling, it was a little as though he had already left us, and was at peace.

'I know,' I said. 'It's all right. And I'm glad we — you — were able to bring him to a place like this to die. It seems more — fitting, somehow.' Fitting, I thought. That was the word *he* had used; an old-fashioned word. 'But he's not a Catholic, Nick.'

Nick turned away from the window to face me, his eyes crinkling at the corners. 'How d'you know, Emma? It's been a long time, hasn't it? And didn't you notice that Brother Crispin knew him? Liked him, too, I'd say. He was certainly distressed to find it was his Mr Kelly.'

My father did not regain consciousness. Nick had been right, according to Doctor Wilde; he was in a coma. But it was another two days and almost three nights before he died. Nick went back to the camp, and to his work, while the kindly Sisters gave me a cell adjoining my father's, and bullied me gently into using it.

He had been given the last rites, and they watched him, I saw, with a very real affection that was quite apart from the devotion allied to their vocation.

Sister Marion called me on the third

morning, well before dawn. Not that it made any difference to *him*, but I was at least able to sit beside his bed and hold his hand between both of mine until she caught my eye, shook her head, and drew the sheet gently over his face.

They were very kind to me; not the least of their kindness being the completely matter-of-fact attitude they held towards death. The Mission possessed its own radio transmitter and messages were sent to Chundi, and to Lowell and Driscoll, giving the date and time of death of their client Andrew Grant Callow, and its cause. Doctor Wilde signed the death certificate and handed it into my keeping to take back with me to Chundi, and asked the Game and Tsetse Department to advise Nick of my father's death when he raised them on the radio later that morning.

He was to be buried that afternoon. 'It's best, you understand, Miss Callow, not to wait too long in these parts.

Come now, and we'll talk about him a little.' Brother Crispin led me along the corridor to a tiny office near the annexe entrance.

My father had reached the very nadir of despair when his second exploration licence expired with little or nothing to show for twenty years of searching for diamonds, he told me.

He had hoped for diamonds of gemstone quality, not the poor, small stones that were fit only for industrial use, which were all that had come his way.

He had wandered up to the Mission one evening, hungry and hopeless, but determined beyond all reason not to go back to Chundi, or Rhodesia, or England. Could not they find him work of some sort? They had taken him in.

Since that time he had tended the Mission's kitchen gardens, overseeing the labour, the painting of the houses and the church whenever necessary, and making himself generally useful. To them, he had always been simply 'Mr

Kelly', a quiet man, who had come to prefer his own company, and so was left pretty much to himself.

'He had one stone,' said Brother Crispin. 'He prized it very much, partly because it was the only one he ever found of any size or value, but mainly I suspect because it helped him to prove something to himself.' His eyes twinkled briefly as he regarded me.

' 'Tis a terrible thing to be searching for something for twenty years of your life and not finding it. For then you begin to feel that you were wrong and everyone else was right, and you've given up everything worthwhile; and for what?'

'But he'd found one, d'you see, and it justified things a trifle to him, I've no doubt. Where there was one, there must be others; he'd just not had the luck to find them.

'It became, I think, his *raison d'etre* for twenty years of lonely searching; for the loss of a wife who couldn't live the kind of life he asked of her — and, God help her, who are we to blame her? — and the penance of never seeing his only child again.'

I cleared my throat. 'He *did* see me, actually. For a moment or so, a few days before he died.'

'Did he now? And know you?'

'He knew who I was — yes.'

'Well, now, I'm glad of that. You'd be a sight for his sore eyes, a fine-looking young woman like you, if I may say so. God's good, d'you see, in ways we don't expect, and never plan for.' He lapsed into silence, toying with the black-and-white bead cross of the rosary about his neck.

'And the diamond he found?' I said at last. 'Did he sell it?' The Brother's eyes met mine speculatively. 'You see, I've been so hoping he didn't if it meant so much to him, but I felt he must have had to, in order to have me traced.'

I told him of the story of my father's visit to the camp, and of the cheque he had sent to Jerry. In fact, encouraged by the kindly interest with which the shrewd grey eyes regarded me, I found myself telling him the whole story; something I had not done, even with Nick. When I spoke of my mother he shook his head.

'Ah, the poor woman. It was no life for her, or for a child, the kind your father expected. He realised that, I fancy, in the end. He became one of us, you know.' He smiled. 'So there we were, calling him Mr Kelly and all, as though he were an Irishman into the bargain. He'd got used to it, d'you see, over the years. Though he made no secret of his identity with us. I suppose he knew it didn't matter to us either way.'

'You mean he became a Catholic?' I stared at him.

'Indeed he did. Some years ago, now. I think he found comfort in it.'

'Yes, of course.' That I could understand. 'But I thought the Church — your Church — didn't recognise divorce?'

'No indeed. But it was your mother

271

who divorced him, and married again. Your father did not. Though it would be hard to discover who was to blame. You must not judge your mother, you know. It was a terrible decision for her to have to make. She did what she thought best for you both, no doubt.'

Again he fell silent, then looked up at me and added: 'No, he didn't sell the diamond. He wouldn't ever part with it. Not that it was so very wonderful.'

'You saw it, then?'

'Indeed I did. But I know little of these things. It looked like a dullish pebble to me, and not so very big at that.

'But there is a Brother here, from South Africa, who knows about diamonds. He said it was a good one — a blue diamond I think he called it.' He shook his head and smiled. 'I could see no blue, nor anything else, much, myself. He took a glass to it, I remember, and said he could find no flaw in it, which pleased your father, and that it might be about a carat weight after it was cut and polished. I think that's what he said.'

I realised, as I listened, that I knew nothing about them either. My mother had inherited my grandmother's diamond solitaire, which had always seemed to me to be a very large stone indeed, and extremely beautiful. I knew it was insured as an eighty-point diamond; that was about all I did know.

'Will you — ' I hesitated. 'Will you keep it, and sell it for whatever purpose you'd like?' My father owed them that, I felt. And surely he'd be glad it had been put to such a use.

The Brother was clearly puzzled. 'We do not have it, Miss Kelly — Callow. In any case,' he spread the hands that lay on his lap. 'Surely it should be your inheritance? And believe me, your father was worthy of his hire. He was as much help to us as we ever were to him. He was not a man to accept charity without doing his utmost to repay it. A proud and independent man, your father, and we have missed him sorely since he went away.'

'Did — did you look for him? When he — when you found his room unoccupied? When did he leave here?' This was a question I had been wishing to put for some time, but had not known how.

'Miss Callow. I see you don't understand. Your father never lived here — never slept here. He took his meals with us, it's true, and he was here every day from just after sunrise until just before dark.' A smile lit his face.

'He shot for us, too. Venison for the pot. He was a wonderful marksman. We have authority, you understand, to kill out game that wanders on to our land, this being a tsetse area. Part of the corridor, in fact. But only according to the rules as laid down in Chundi. Light game can be shot with a .270, but heavy game never with less than a .375 and an authorised hunter must be employed. Your father was such a one, and this helped us enormously in the feeding of staff and patients.

'Before then we had tended to rely on the kindness of the field officers from nearby camps in supplying us periodically from their kill. For obvious reasons this was not a reliable source. Your father saved us a great deal of expense in many ways, I can assure you. He would never take payment, but whenever Father Bryant went into Chundi he paid a little into his account there, and told him so.'

He waited, quietly, watching me from under the bushy grey brows, seeing my puzzlement.

'But then, where *did* he live? He could never have come here every day from the rondavel where Mr Locke and I found him, and walked back at night. It's *much* too far away; almost as far as the camp. It's on the other side of the river, too.'

'From his house, of course; where else?'

House, I thought. 'I must go back to the house — ' 'Can no longer reach the house to wash.'

275

'Of course,' I said at last. 'I — I thought he meant here. That is, after we came and you told us that you knew him. D'you know where it is?'

He nodded. 'After the funeral I will find someone to take you there. We sent two of the staff to look for him, you understand, in case he was ill. He was subject to bad bouts of malaria.

'But when they came back and reported the house empty we didn't worry; or not at first.'

He leaned forward earnestly. 'You must understand, Miss Callow, that your father had become something of a recluse; almost a hermit.' He smiled. 'The Church tends to understand this kind of compulsion, you know. We ourselves go on retreat at least once yearly. We suspected that there were times when he could bear to see nobody; when he wandered off into the bush — perhaps making a sort of pilgrimage over ground he had trodden for so many years before the diamond bug finally burnt itself out.

If it ever really did.

'We left him in peace, you understand, and asked him no questions. Anything he told us, he told us of his own accord. And that was very little.'

He rose. 'And now you must excuse me, my child. I must get back to the presbytery; there's a clinic in a few minutes. The Sisters will see to your wants; don't be afraid to ask them for anything. And Sister Marion will bring you to the church for the Requiem Mass.'

I saw Nick again that afternoon, for the first time since he had driven away after leaving me with my father at the Mission. He came into the little church quietly, and sat down beside me on the hard bench at the front near my father's coffin.

It was not, somehow, a sombre service. Father O'Halloran said the Mass in a voice that was light, and full of hope, so that the beautiful words lingered on in my mind after he had spoken them:

— 'Command the holy angels to
— lead him to the home of Paradise —
— 'Brethren, we will not have you
ignorant concerning them that are
asleep, that you be not sorrowful — '

The sun was shining when we went
outside to follow my father on his last
journey to the little cemetery behind
the church. Nick assisted in carrying
the coffin, almost as though he had
arranged it beforehand. The sky above
the Mission was a deep and glorious
blue, though far away, towards the
camp, mushrooms of grey cloud gathered low on the horizon.

And then it was over. I dropped my
handful of earth into the grave and
stepped back, dry-eyed, for Nick to do
the same. Then we walked quietly back
to the presbytery and to Father
O'Halloran's tiny office for tea and
biscuits, and ordinary casual conversation.

11

I thought that perhaps Brother Crispin had forgotten his promise to find someone to show me the way to my father's house, as the afternoon ticked by and he did not reappear.

Finally, Nick rose, and came across to where I stood talking with Sister Marion and Father O'Halloran about the floods that beset the lower parts of the plain surrounding the Mission once the rainy season got under way.

'You're coming back to the camp with me, of course, Emma?' he asked as the nun and priest excused themselves and moved away. 'We should leave soon to get back in daylight, and I've been ordered back to Chundi tomorrow. Apparently there's real rain on the way, and I only cover the corridor in the dry season.'

'Yes, of course. I remember your

telling me.' Suddenly, we might have been strangers standing there. He had seen me through, from the beginning to the end; from the finding of my father to the final, irrevocable losing of him; and now it was over.

Now we would go back to Chundi, where we would murmur polite good-byes and I would thank him for all the acts of kindness that he appeared to scatter about like confetti wherever he went, and catch the next plane to a world so far removed from this that it might well be the moon.

The fact that this was how it must be held no comfort for me. And yet, I told myself, within a week of sitting at my desk and grappling once again with Mr Mostyn's eccentricities, *this* was the world that would become as distant as the moon; *this* the unreal interlude that had interrupted, for such a brief time, the quiet, uneventful tenor of my days.

I was wondering how to tell him that first I had a pilgrimage of my own to make when Brother Crispin appeared.

'If you'll come now, Miss Callow, I've a guide for you. John here knows where to find the house.' He glanced from me to Nick, and said: 'You'll be going back just now with Mr Locke?' I nodded, and turned to Nick.

'It's father's house,' I said. 'Where he was living — until he became so sick, I suppose. It's near here, Brother Crispin says. It's just that I wanted to see it.'

'I'll come along and follow you down just now,' promised the Brother. 'You'll be needing to tell me what about his things. Any small articles you'll be wanting to keep you can take in Mr Locke's Land-Rover, and the rest can be brought into Chundi whenever we're going through, and sent on to you. So you'd better take John and drive down where he tells you, Mr Locke.'

We drove back across the plain and along the main road for a few hundred yards, until John, sitting, black and jovial, at Nick's elbow, pointed ahead.

'It's a track down there, boss. You go there.'

We bumped and jolted our way from the comparative smoothness of the road on to the rutted but surprisingly wide track he indicated, and down a sharp incline between the trees. At the bottom of the dip the road began to curve sharply eastwards, and it was at this point that we saw the river, narrow here, but swift, flowing beside it. I think Nick was as surprised as I was.

'Can't be the same river,' he muttered as he braked, too narrow. 'Besides — '

'Same river, boss,' said John decisively. 'Is bridge just along. You drive on now and I show you.'

He was right. Within less than a mile we came across it; a rough concrete structure carefully placed to span the river at its narrowest point.

Nick eyed it dubiously. 'A home-made job if ever I saw one,' he remarked. 'Looks as though it was put together with a knife and fork. Hope it'll hold.'

'Yes, boss. Will hold. Long time here.'

Nick grunted. 'I don't see much recommendation in that. However, here goes then, John, and on your own head be it. Or over it, if we sink.'

There were about six inches to spare on either side, and no parapet. My heart was in my mouth as Nick inched the Land-Rover across and up the sharply-inclined ramp at the other side. He let out his breath, murmured 'Thank God for that,' in a heartfelt whisper, and continued on between the curving track lined with trees, or shrubs, symmetrically placed, it seemed, and with smooth, rubbery branches that spread at strange, contorted angles from the spindly trunks. Circlets of pointed leaves decorated the tips of the branches only, and here and there a small, yellowish-white bud seemed about to burst open.

'Nick,' I said. I must have whispered, for he did not reply.

'Nick.' I touched his arm. 'Could — can we stop here?' He glanced at me curiously, then braked and waited, long brown hands resting on the wheel.

'What is it, Emma?'

I pointed. 'Are they called frangipani? Those shrubs?'

'That's right. Someone must have planted them in a semi-circular drive, years ago.'

'My father. *He* planted them.' My voice rose. 'I don't know how I know, but I do.' I pushed the door open and began to climb down on to the track.

'Emma. Come back. Mind those buffalo beans. Oh, for heaven's sake! We don't know how far it is — '

'*I* do. It's just ahead. You'll see it if you just drive on.' I began to run. I think he called after me again, but I did not turn, and after a moment I heard the Land-Rover's engine as he started after me.

Almost immediately, as I rounded the bend, the rough driveway widened out into a forecourt of sorts, and then I saw the house.

It appeared to be resting on stilts; then I saw that the base, for a depth of about two feet, was of rough, probably locally made brick, and that the frame house stood high upon it.

The red paint had all but peeled away from its corrugated-iron roof. There was no porch, the half-gauzed wooden door fitting flush with the screened veranda. The wood of the inner wall was exposed in places where the once-yellow colour wash had cracked and peeled away. The inner door was ajar.

I heard the Land-Rover pull up behind me, but ignored it. As one in a dream, I walked across the veranda, through the open doorway and along the narrow, clapboarded hall to the door on the left. There was a floral-patterned, porcelain knob, cracked in places, that it did not surprise me at all to recognise.

I opened the door, crossed the room and looked about me; first at the narrow bed, stripped to its faded mattress, then at the window set in the sloping roof.

I think I heard Nick's arrival in the

doorway, but still I did not turn. Instead, I dropped to my knees on the bare strip-boarded flooring, running my fingers along one of the grooves to where it met the wall.

'She had the better of her mother there, in her own small way.' I may have said it aloud, because Nick strode forward until he was beside me, then lowered himself on to the edge of the bed.

'Emma,' he said gently. 'What are you — remembering?'

I looked up at him then, smiling happily, like a child. 'My rainbow candles,' I said. 'I put them in here — under this board. It moves, you see? I wonder if they're still — '

'No, Emma. They'll have rotted, or white ant will have dealt with them long ago.'

'But my father knew, so he must have found them; it's the only way he *could* know. Mother wouldn't let me take them. She told me to throw them away, so I hid them in my secret place. I remember, Nick. I remember now.'

He stooped and ran a hand over my hair. 'You must have been a ghastly child. But that would be a long time ago, you know. They'll be gone now, my dear.'

'See,' I said, ignoring him, 'there's the gap. You slide your hand in like this — '

'Not any more you don't.' Nick, watching my efforts, began to laugh. 'You've grown a bit since then, remember.'

Then he saw my crestfallen expression. 'Here, let me.'

'If my hand won't go in, yours *certainly* won't,' I retorted, with such an indignant return to my earlier loftiness of manner that he let out a hoot of laughter.

'No, but my fingers are longer. There'll be nothing there, I promise you, apart from the odd dead bat, or shrew, or shed snake skin.'

He laid down on the floor beside me, nevertheless, so that our shoulders were touching in the narrow space between bed and window, and began to probe the dark, dusty cavity with his fingers. I saw him check, stoop lower to peer inside, then he lifted his head and looked at me.

'I don't know about candles,' he said. 'But there's certainly something there. And it looks as though the board was moved and replaced fairly recently.' His face wore an odd expression, and as our eyes met it was as though the same thought had communicated itself to us simultaneously.

'Let me — ' I began. He shook his head. 'No. There can only be joists down there, then the concrete foundations below. The place is built almost entirely of wood — he'd have had to build it over concrete and put in a lead ant course or it would have crumbled to dust long ago. As it is — ' He pressed a thumb along the skirting. 'It's gone in places; even with him living in it and spraying the place from time to time. They always win in the end.'

He levered himself on to his feet.

'Back in a minute. What we need are pincers — something like that. Don't touch it now or you'll knock it off.'

I waited, sitting on my hands on the dusty floor, staring first at the ticking of the mattress, then at the yellow-washed wall, and the ridges that revealed the planking, while a sense of wonder pervaded my whole being, and a quarter of a century rolled away.

Jim Stone, I had thought he said. Far away, at the back of my mind, the name had lingered on as that of a sinister being who had lured my father away from my mother and me, that night, and prevented him from ever returning. Jim Stone. Gemstone.

Yet I had not been so far wrong after all, young as I was. The one and only diamond of gemstone quality had been found by him that very day; hence his feverish excitement and my mother's desperation as she foresaw the years of arid, comfortless existence stretching out endlessly before her while he spent his days chasing his dream. 'Jim Stone' had certainly lured him away; from both of us. Poor Mother.

The diamond lay in a tiny box which my father had wrapped in tinfoil. As I pulled it away a flimsy piece of ruled paper — the kind one might tear from a pocket diary — fell out.

'Not your candles, Emma. They're all gone. But if you take this, and have it cut and polished, you'll find all your rainbow colours in it. With all my love, Daddy.' I had barely finished reading it when we heard the crunch of Brother Crispin's Land-Rover outside.

★ ★ ★

There was very little arranging to do. Brother Crispin gratefully accepted my offer of the furniture for the Mission, and there was little else, apart from my delighted discovery of a small hoard of photographs of a toddler, and of a small girl with her hand in my father's

When I came through to show them to Nick I found him peering down the sights of one of my father's rifles. He had found three of them, and was handling them lovingly.

He looked up at me and smiled. 'Beautiful,' he said. 'Cleaned and oiled, and cared for, all of them. He wouldn't be the one to keep them any other way, of course.'

'What's that one you're holding? It looks like Greg's.'

'M'mm. A .404. Beautiful. And there's a .375 and .270 here.'

'Have *you* got one? A .404?'

'What? No, mine's a .375. It's Government's anyway, actually.'

'Take it then, Nick.'

He coloured and put it down hastily. 'Emma, don't be idiotic. A thing like this costs a bomb. If you sell it — '

'I don't want to sell it. I want to give it to you. And the others too, if they'll be of any use to you. If not, *you* sell them.'

He rested a hand, briefly and reverently, upon the .404, then thrust both hands deep into his pockets, and frowned furiously at me.

'Look, Emma, if you think you have to *pay* me anything just because I happened to be around when — '

'Stop it, Nick. It's you who are being idiotic. What d'you think I'm going to do with these in England, for heaven's sake? Pot at pigeons in Trafalgar Square? I'd — I'd *like* you to have them. Please.'

We stood for a moment regarding each other in silence while I willed him to say yes. That way, at least, he'd have something to remember me by. He'd be able, some day, to recount to his wife, or to his sons, how he had come by them. I could almost hear him saying it: 'Queer story altogether. There was this girl — well, woman really. Nearly thirty, she was. City type, and uppish, rather. Bit on the cold side; you know? No, darling, not my kind at all. Career woman, I'd imagine. Completely out of place in the middle of Africa. Cool, and tall, and — yes — elegant; I'll give her that, too. Then there was this queer bod who turned out to be her father. Quite bonkers in a harmless kind of way. Bushed, you know?'

Well, it would be better than nothing. At least he'd *remember* me.

He cleared his throat. 'Well,' he said at last, embarrassed. 'I suppose — Well. No, you wouldn't find much use for them behind a city desk.' He paused, as though waiting for me to say something, but I couldn't. Instead, I just shook my head and smiled.

'Well, I — it's a terrific gift, Emma. I'll treasure them, you know that. And think of you every time I handle them.'

Yes, I said silently. Do that, Nick; that's what I gave them to you for.

'We'd better go. It's a long haul back, and as it is we'll be driving part of the way in the dark.'

He led the way outside. Brother Crispin had already gone, taking John with him. I looked about me at the curving driveway, the frangipanis, and then beyond the forecourt to where the drive continued, and said: 'It isn't, you know.'

'Isn't what?'

'A long haul. The drive continues on down there, following the river more or less, until it reaches the rondavel, where it narrows into the track that leads to the camp. About ten miles all told, I'd say. Not much more.'

He stared at me, then at the drive, then looked about him, thinking.

'The direction's right,' he said at last. 'But as for the road continuing — ' He laughed. 'Very unlikely, Emma. Anyway, how d'you know?'

'I don't know how I know. I only know I do.' As I spoke I seemed to see my father's halting writing: 'Have come to rondavel to be nearer.' I had to be right. As he hesitated, I added impatiently: 'At least *try* it, Nick.' I *had* to go that way. I was sure I'd been there before.

'And if it peters out and we have to come back?'

'We won't. And if it rains before we get back, and it looks as if it might, just think how much easier than battling your way across the ghastly bridge again, driving all those miles along the Chundi road and crawling up through the bush to the camp.'

It was that, I think, that decided him. The clouds were gathering ominously ahead of us, though the sun still shone and the sky above our heads was the same vivid blue. He nodded. 'Right. Got everything you want to take?'

'Yes,' I said briefly, and swung myself into the Land-Rover. There was time for only one backward glance at the house before the bend in the drive hid it from view.

The road was rutted but easily negotiable. It did not peter out, and the river was clearly visible on our right for most of the way.

We travelled in silence, Nick glancing at me from time to time as though about to speak, then thinking better of it.

I was glad of the silence. I was using it to condition myself to the fact that this interlude in my life was nearly over.

Tomorrow we would travel back to Chundi. An hour or so the following morning with Mr Jerome Driscoll to attend to the legalities pertaining to my father's death would complete my business in Chundi, and I would be free to leave Minzanda on the first available flight.

Thirteen days ago I had never heard of Nicholas Locke, B.V.M. & S.; M.R.C.V.S.; was not aware that he existed. There was no problem. All I had to do was to forget him. It's all in the mind, Emma, I told myself. Once you're back in England it will fade from your memory in no time; you'll see.

When he stopped the Land-Rover I was so far away that at first I was not aware of the lack of motion. He ran a finger down my cheek. 'Wake up,' he said. 'Come on. I want to show you something.'

We were on fairly high ground, and a coppery-brown anthill rose on our right. He took my hand, pulling me up behind him.

The clouds had separated about us, and as I looked around I saw what he was showing me. At intervals along the horizon curtains of grey cloud hung from the sky to the ground; some near at hand, others several miles distant. The sun, still several weeks from its meridian, was now low in the sky to the north-west, and as I watched a rainbow began to form over Diamond Hill; a beautiful, clear arc of colour that looked close enough for me to reach out and touch it where the curve slanted in our direction.

'Just about over the house, I'd say,' remarked Nick, pointing. 'If not actually inside it, as your father said you used to think. D'you remember that, Emma?'

I shook my head. 'No,' I said regretfully. 'I remember very little, really, you know.'

'That's because your memories were not kept alive for you. That's the way one does forget.'

I only hope you're right, I thought,

and began to feel a little better. If that was all it took —

'All the same, you did remember something. This road, for instance. You must have come down here often, as a child, with your father. To the rondavel, perhaps.'

'He built that first. My mother told me that, though. I didn't actually remember it. At least I don't think — ' I hesitated. 'But I see now, why she didn't. Keep my memories alive, I mean. I — I've blamed my mother, ever since I learnt that my father was alive all these years and she never told me. But now, I don't think I blame her any more. She couldn't have been expected to bear it.'

He did not reply, and when I looked up it was to find him frowning thoughtfully into the distance.

We stood for a moment longer, watching the rainbow grow stronger, and then fade until it disappeared completely, and continued on our way, past the rondavel as I had foretold, and on up to the camp. We were back well before nightfall.

* * *

Driving into Chundi late the following afternoon held for me a little of the sensation of arriving in some great metropolis. Amused, I remarked to Nick that had I, at that moment, been required to cross a busy London street, my courage might well have failed me.

He laughed. 'You're bushed,' he said. 'That's what's the matter with you. Cheer up. It won't last long.' He paused, then added: 'You must be itching to get back to civilisation, all the same.'

As I did not know quite how to reply to this, I was more than thankful that the Land-Rover drew up, at that precise moment, in Blake's forecourt.

He climbed out with me in spite of my protestations that it was really not necessary, and stood for a moment supervising Thomas's unloading of my

299

gear from the back of the vehicle. Then he took my arm and led me inside.

'Come on,' he said. 'Buy you a drink. You need it after all that, and I'm gasping for a beer.'

I was greeted with touching pleasure and courtesy by the reception clerk, who assured me I would find my rondavel in perfect order and handed me my key without having to look up the number.

I glanced around me, feeling the slight bewilderment and time-slip sensation that comes to a traveller from too much happening in too short a time.

'It seems ages — I mean *years* — since I first stood here. It *can't* be less than a fortnight.' I tried to laugh. 'I feel like an exile returning home. It has that sort of ancient familiarity about it.'

'It's ancient all right.' He took my elbow and led me into the lounge. 'What'll you drink? If you're as dry as I am you'd better have a lager.'

There had been rain in Chundi, the bar waiter informed us; two heavy

300

storms that had delighted the farming community. It was certainly cooler, and I remarked upon this to Nick.

'Yes, It'll hot up again before the next storm, though. Always does.'

The rapport between us was gone. There seemed nothing whatever to talk about. Nick sat opposite me, twisting the stem of his glass and staring thoughtfully into the contents as though his thirst had quite deserted him.

'Let's see,' he said at last, abruptly. 'I'll be seeing Jerry this evening some time. Would you like me to fix an appointment for you tomorrow?'

'Thank you.' I thought of Jerry Driscoll, and the conversation I had overheard between him and Nick before leaving Chundi for the valley. At least, Nick no longer believed that it was diamonds, and not my father, that I had been seeking; whatever Jerry Driscoll thought. And then, as sometimes disastrously happens when one's mind is following a certain channel, I found myself saying: 'Tell him I managed to garner one fair-sized diamond for my pains;' and could have bitten out my tongue in dismay at my appalling slip.

Nick did not get it at first. The silver-grey eyes met mine, the dark brows drawn together above them in the now-familiar frown, while I sought frantically for something to say that would divert his thoughts before the light dawned.

Of course I could think of nothing. I saw the flash of comprehension in his eyes, and watched the dark flush mount in his cheeks, and slowly recede, so frozen with horror at my stupidity that I was unable, even, to look away.

He picked up his glass and drained it. Then he rose, smiled, nodded, said: 'Well, better be getting along, I suppose. 'Bye, Emma,' and walked away. I sat as though rooted to the spot, listening to the thrum of the Land-Rover's engine as he started it up, and hearing it fade until it merged with the sound of the street traffic, and he had finally, irrevocably gone.

★ ★ ★

I rang Lowell and Driscoll the following morning to discover that, true to his word, Nicholas Locke had arranged an appointment for me at ten o'clock. I followed the clerk into Jerry's office in some trepidation. Nick was sure to have told his friend that their summing-up of my character, and of my motives in seeking my father, had been overheard by me, and I was dreading the encounter.

True to type, moreover, I reacted, as I had reacted all my life to embarrassing or humiliating situations, by entering his office wearing a frozen mask instead of a face, and replying to his greetings and words of sympathy regarding my father's death in monosyllables that tinkled on the air like icicles. I pretended, even, not to see his outstretched hand; my own were shaking slightly, and I had no intention of letting him know it.

There was not a great deal to discuss. I made it quite clear that the sum of money that the White Fathers had set aside for my father was to be returned to them with a letter expressing my desire that they should have it. I would be writing to them myself, I told him, as soon as I got back to England, to thank them for all their many kindnesses.

Then I realised that I did not know where to send the letter. Surely there could be no deliveries to such an outpost?

Jerry grinned. 'White Fathers, Back of Beyond — Something like that? No; actually you address it care of Private Bag, Chundi. They'll get it. It's the only way the farmers — or any of 'em out there — can get any mail. Whoever comes into Chundi picks up the bag and takes it out. Some rent a box of their own, and come in once a week to collect it. But not many.'

I had to admit that there was no sign, in his manner, that Nick had told him of my inadvertent eavesdropping. There was instead a warmth about it that actually thawed my own a little, and he lost no time in letting me know he had heard about what he called my 'marvellous feat of markmanship' with the buffalo.

'You could have fooled me,' he said, his eyes travelling over my crisp London suit and newly-washed hair. 'When are you thinking of flying back, Miss Callow?'

So I was Miss Callow again. Did that mean that Nick had told him? I must, moreover, have looked rather as if I had deliberately dressed that morning to fill the role he had previously chosen for me, which meant that my very appearance made me a stranger once more. I had sorted through my limited wardrobe, packing this and discarding that, seeking the correct wear for a woman keeping an appointment with a lawyer on a warm, sunny morning in the middle of Africa.

Then I had come upon my laundered suit and thought: to hell with it. To hell with images, and conformity, and trying to fit myself into a mould. I'm Emma Callow, I'm nearly thirty, I'm over-tall and over-fastidious about my person because with my build I can't afford not to be.

To my mother I'm angular, unwomanly and gauche; to my father I was 'like a goddess'. To Jerry Driscoll I'm a hardbitten career woman with an eye to the main chance; to Nick, for a fleeting moment (though it was almost certainly pure kindness allied to emotional reaction that induced him to say it) I was a brave and beautiful girl. To Dora Bannister I was somebody one engaged in friendly conversation at first sight, called 'love', and kissed warmly on the cheek. Perhaps I was all of them, at one time or another; perhaps none. One thing certain, however; from now on I was going to try to be *me*; whatever that was.

I drew a deep breath. 'Jerry,' I said. 'I want to tell you something.'

He heard me out in complete silence, patches of colour flowing and receding

306

in his cheeks as he listened, jaw slightly dropped. It was all too obvious to me that Nick had told him nothing after all. ' — So you see, I wanted to let you know the way it really was, because I let it slip, accidentally, to Nick, that I had overheard you.

'I never meant to eavesdrop, but,' I grinned at him and he smiled back at me, albeit a trifle weakly, 'you know what they say about eavesdroppers, so I suppose it served me right.

'You were quite justified in drawing your own conclusions; you were simply concerned for my father. I just wanted you to know that it doesn't matter at all — that I'm grateful for the effort you and Nick put into finding me when he asked you to. You've all — ' There was a lump in my throat which I firmly swallowed. 'Everyone I've met in the two weeks I've been here has been the soul of kindness to me. I just wanted to say thank you.' All the old warmth was back in his eyes as he stretched out a hand across the desk towards me, and I thought; thank God, that's all right, then. As far as Jerry's concerned at any rate.

As for Nick, it as probably better as it was. Far better not to meet again. And Jerry would tell him what I had said, so that, after all, he might not think too badly of me.

★   ★   ★

It was dim in Blake's foyer after the glare of the street, so that I did not at first recognise the woman who rose and walked towards me as I crossed to the desk for my key. Then as I turned I saw something dangling from her hand. It was a cat basket.

'Hello, love.' She reached up and planted a kiss on my cheek. 'It's good to see you again. I'm sorry about your Dad.'

I had long given up wondering how everyone in Minzanda managed to find out everything about everybody else in less time than it would have taken to telegraph the information at home. I was far too glad to see Dora again to care anyway. She was all I had left in Minzanda, now.

I embraced her warmly. 'Nick let you take him?' I gestured towards the basket.

'Yes. Well, he left word that I could. He's gone up the line.' I had already understood this expression to refer to the up-country line of rail which served the farming community.

'There's a suspected outbreak of contagious bovine pleuro-pneumonia at Linden's farm. Only hope it doesn't find its way down here, that's all.'

'Did you come here especially to see me, Dora?' I found the thought oddly cheering; the more so as Nick was not even in Chundi. I had been comforting myself with the thought that at least his physical presence was no more than half-a-mile away from me while I remained at Blake's. And as it was —

'Of course I did. Wanted to know when you're flying out. Because you've missed today's flight, so Frank and I thought it would be nice if you came to us for the rest of your stay. We've plenty of room.'

'Oh, but — ' I had done nothing, yet, about flight arrangements. 'Is there a flight every day?'

'Not quite. There's one tomorrow, and on Friday, then none until Monday.'

'Friday. I could make that easily, that's if there's a seat.' Nick might be back by then, so —

'There'll be a seat, all right. And we can drive you to the airport. Come on, then. Let's see about your things.'

I think the two days I spent with the Bannisters did more to reorientate me than anything else could have done, just then, and their warm friendliness worked wonders for my morale at a time when I needed it most.

I left without seeing Nick again. Now, however, I was better able to view this circumstance as the blessing it undoubtedly was. I did not know how much Dora suspected of my feelings towards him, but his name cropped up with almost monotonous regularity as I gave her the details of my few days with him in the valley, so that she must inevitably have drawn a few conclusions. I was quite past caring, I found. Incredible that I could change so much in so short a time.

They saw me on to the aircraft on Friday morning, my address safely written down in Dora's diary because, she said, she intended to write to me, and in any case they would certainly look me up when next in England. I had made two staunch friends from my pilgrimage to Africa, at any rate.

I had wired Mother at Fleetchurch to tell her I was on my way home, but that I did not know what time I would arrive at Heathrow; feeling that, in this way, everyone would be let off the hook with regard to the question of meeting me. It was a trying journey from Fleetchurch and, in any case, I wanted, first, the privacy of my own flat. I told myself I would ring when I got there and arrange to go down for the weekend; I had my peace to make with them there, and my conscience would not let me delay it.

Sleet was falling when I touched down at Heathrow two days after leaving Chundi's grilling sunshine, and the sky was a cold, leaden grey. I had left England on a warm, autumn morning less than three weeks ago; now it was already winter. I sat huddled in my inadequate topcoat all the way to Victoria Air Terminal, and grabbed the first taxi I could find to my flat in Kentish Town. By the time I arrived my hands were so numb that I could scarcely thrust the key into the lock.

The hall was dark, cold and unwelcoming; my small refrigerator empty and inactive as I had left it. I switched on lights, fire, and water heater, then realised wretchedly that I had forgotten to buy even the barest necessities in the way of food, and was far too chilled and weary to venture out in search of any.

Dully I filled the kettle and plugged it in, groped in the kitchen drawer for a tin-opener, and dropped to my haunches to view the contents of my tiny store cupboard.

I was home again.

12

Life settled into the old pattern; or almost. I found myself going down more often to Fleetchurch; at first because I was lonely, I think. Later, it occurred to me that my mother became progressively more eager to see me, though I could not think why at the time.

I told her little about my father, at first, apart from the fact of his death. As time went on, however, she began to question me more closely about the period I had spent in Minzanda. I answered all her questions, avoiding nothing; not even the pain of mentioning Nick.

Allan had been unaffectedly glad to see me back. He hugged and kissed me in a way he had never done before.

'Thought perhaps you'd taken against us,' he muttered gruffly. 'Especially your mother. She's been upset about it, Emma. Don't think she hasn't.'

I wrote to Dora, and the White Fathers. Then, a little nearer Christmas; not so near as to make it seem like a Christmas letter, nor yet so soon as to appear to be pursuing him, I wrote my masterpiece to Nicholas Locke.

It really was a masterpice, of its kind. It took me three whole evenings to write, and almost my entire pad of airmail paper. Friendly in tone, I thought, but not too friendly. Expressing gratitude, but without fulsomeness. Nothing austere of course, but with no trace of over-familiarity; or indeed, any suggestion at all that he had been more than a congenial and helpful companion for the few short days during which he and I had been thrown rather closer together, both physically and emotionally, than strangers usually are. It was essential that I make it clear to him that I had read nothing more into our brief relationship than that.

As might be supposed, the result of these labours resembled a not-very-enthusiastic letter of the type one might write to one's hostess after a dull and rather boring weekend, but I had not the heart to try again. It was the kind of letter no one in his right mind would consider it necessary to acknowledge. Nick did not acknowledge it.

My brother Brian, at a loose end until the New Year, when he was to go up to Cambridge, took to visiting his bird of the moment, who had taken a job in the City, in midweek and spending the night on my settee. He helped to take the sting out of my sudden, inexpressible loneliness and so was welcome, in spite of astronomical inroads upon my larder.

I went home for Christmas. On Boxing Day, during a morning walk through the park, Dominic Trafford at last asked me to marry him. I thanked him as gracefully as I knew how, and told him I feared I was becoming too attached to my bachelor-girl status to think of marrying.

There was a look in his eye as he regarded me that I was never quite sure was not due — in part at any rate — to relief.

'I shall ask you again,' he assured me, however, as we parted amicably at my stepfather's gate.

Mother was alone, Allan and Brian having strolled down to a neighbouring friend's house for a game of snooker. She was embroidering a piece of tapestry, a pastime she was fond of. As I entered the living room she looked up, and our eyes met. Our sex being the uncanny one that it is at times, it was immediately clear to me that she knew Dominic had just proposed.

I grinned at her. 'I said no,' I told her.

'Oh, Emma, you didn't.'

'What about lunch? Shall I start carving the turkey? It'll save Allan — '

'No. Wait.' I hesitated, saw the appeal in her eyes, and went over to sit on the rug at her feet. It was all too easy for me to tower over her, even sitting in a chair.

'Emma, there's something different

about you.' She put her needlework aside and looked down into my face, studying me as though searching for something. 'You're — I don't know how to put it — gentler, or sadder, or something. You will never know how I dreaded that first meeting after you came back from Minzanda. I dreaded your anger more than you'll ever realise.'

I smiled at her. 'I had no idea I was such a shrew.'

'No, I'm serious. I — Allan and I talked about things while you were away. We decided we'd been wrong in denying your own father's existence to you all these years. I just want to say I'm sorry, Emma. Did we hurt you very much? We never meant to, you know. We meant it all for the best.'

I put my arm about her shoulders. 'It's all right,' I said. 'I saw him, and he saw me. I saw a great many other things, too. I saw that no young girl, with a small child to bring up, could have lived the kind of life he asked of you. You were quite right to leave him.

Don't worry any more about it.'

'But you think I ought to have told you — ?'

I hesitated. I was no longer sure, even, of that. Who was I to know what was right and what was wrong? I gave her shoulders a gentle squeeze. 'I think we all have to do what we think is best at the time. What else *can* we do?'

There was a softening in her expression. 'Thank you, Emma.' Then she added a little wistfully, 'Is that why you've refused Dominic? And who's that best for — you or him?'

I leapt hurriedly to my feet. 'I don't know. Him, I think.'

'But why, Emma? Oh, why? Is — is there anyone else?'

'Queueing up to marry me, you mean?' I laughed lightly. 'Not that I know of. Cheer up, Mother; he's going to ask me again. So he says.' I made my escape to the kitchen and began to carve the cold turkey and ham for lunch, reflecting that I had answered her truthfully enough. There *was* no one else; never would be, now, for me. So why insult poor Dominic by taking him as second-best?

★ ★ ★

Winter seemed the longest I had ever known. In January I went down with flu, and Allan drove up to fetch me and take me home to Fleetchurch.

Mother was wonderful. Their kindness — hers and Allan's — was such that I kept bursting into tears at the thought of my ingratitude and wretchedness of spirit in spite of all they did. Dominic dashed in to see me when he could — usually at dinner-time as he was rushed off his feet. His father was down with it, too.

Somehow I recovered sufficiently to drag myself back to London and the office; to a querulous Mr Mostyn, a bare half-complement of staff, and battle on.

The first Friday following my return to work was without doubt the worst day of all. It was bitterly cold and the rain fell incessantly; icy rods of rain that beat against chest and shoulders like steel spikes.

It was my weekend shopping day. I had still not fully regained my old vigour, and intended to stock myself up for the weekend and never more venture forth until Monday morning.

The supermarket was crammed with people as drenched and bone-weary as myself. Trollies collided, umbrellas prodded, and toddlers bawled with self-pity. By the time I had collected the necessary amount of sustenance to see me through the weekend I felt like joining them.

The bus does not run along my road, and it proved impossible, upon alighting, to put up my umbrella with a handbag under one arm and a large paper bag of groceries in the other. By the time I reached my door my face and hair were streaming, and the brown paper bag had become dangerously soggy.

And I needed my key. If I hitched the bag over it would probably split. Even if

I stooped, ever so gently, and laid it on the step —

It was the only thing to do, however. The doorway seemed extra dark for some reason and I glanced briefly behind me to see if the street light on the opposite pavement was functioning. Then, as I began to crouch, umbrella, groceries and handbag encumbering me, a long, black shadow detached itself from the shallow porch and a voice said: 'Need any help?'

It was Nick.

I am fairly sure I was weeping by the time we had found our way inside, because I remember thinking gratefully that my face was so wet already that it probably wouldn't show.

He had taken my handbag from me, extracted the key, opened the door, slid the groggy brown paper mess dexterously from my arm into his own, and followed me through into the kitchen, miraculously finding and switching on lights as he went.

Then, dumping everything on to the

counter, he took my umbrella from me and began to unbutton my raincoat.

'You're soaked,' he said accusingly. 'Wringing damn' wet.'

I started to laugh. 'So are you.' His hair hung, glistening and lank, across his forehead, even the silvergrey streak subdued with moisture, and rain was dripping from his nose and chin on to his sodden macintosh.

'That porch of yours is only fit for a dwarf,' he muttered querulously. 'Been waiting for hours. Thought you must have gone down to your mother's for the weekend.'

He blinked the raindrops from his lashes and regarded me steadily for a moment from the silvery eyes beneath wet, jutting brows. The crease between them was suddenly very noticeable.

'Well, Emma Jane Callow,' he said at last, 'can you live without me? Because I can't bloody well live without you, and what's more, I'm sick of trying.'

I don't remember saying anything except 'Oh, Nick,' until he shook me suddenly — and none too gently — by the shoulders and repeated fiercely: 'Well, can you? *Can* you?'

To which I replied: 'No, Nick,' with such rare submissiveness that he actually held me at arm's length and eyed me suspiciously.

And then we were clamped together, sodden raincoats squelching, our mouths locked, raindrops mingling with my tears while we clung to each other like a couple of shipwrecked mariners.

★ ★ ★

I bathed and then prepared a meal while Nick showered and donned a dressing-gown of Brian's that revealed a rather larger amount of hirsute thigh than was strictly *de rigueur*, and I hung his dripping trousers on the rack above the heater.

He watched me as I carried the tray into the living room and set it on the table by the fire.

'Whose dressing-gown did you say this was?'

'Brian's. I told you.'

'H'm. Are you sure?'

I began to giggle helplessly. 'Oh, Nick. If you only knew. How can I tell you? How can I make you — ?'

He reached out and seized my wrist. 'Come and show me instead,' he said. 'And I'm warning you, I intend to take a lot of convincing.'

I dodged his other hand and sat firmly down on the other side of the fireplace.

'We're going to eat,' I said. 'And *then* we'll talk. And who are you to cast aspersions on my virtue when you never wrote, never even told me you — you couldn't live without me?'

He grinned at me. 'Snooty old Emma. I love you when you take that lofty tone. The answer to the first is that judging from your letter I thought you never wanted to hear from me — or of me — again. As to the second, it looked as though I was going to have to, and how did I know I couldn't till I tried?'

'Eat your dinner. It's getting cold.' We ate, dreamily, staring at each other, then down at our plates, like a couple of bemused idiots.

'But you never even hinted how you felt,' I said at last, when I could bear it no longer.

'How could I? With you suddenly being so understanding after all about your mother leaving your father, and — damn it, Emma, I didn't think I had a hope. You can be a frosty little baggage when you like, you know. Then, when you let it out, at Blake's, that you'd overheard Jerry and me discussing you — '

'I never meant to. I swear I didn't. It just — slipped out.'

'Well, I thought you'd done it deliberately. To let me know where I stood in case I got ideas.'

'But I *told* Jerry. I explained it all to him.'

Nick laid down his fork. The familiar crease was back between his brows.

'I didn't see Jerry. There was this outbreak of C.B.P. up the line, and I didn't get back to Chundi until nearly a

326

month after you'd gone; only to find Jerry away in Johannesburg at some legal get-together.

'They told me at Blake's that you'd stayed the last two days at Dora's, so I went out there and got your address. Then your letter came and — ' He lifted a hand and let it fall. 'I decided I'd been an idiot even to hope. It was obviously no go.'

He rose, moved the table aside, reached for me again and pulled me on his knee. I tucked my head against his shoulder and he thrust his fingers through my hair.

'Nearly dry. Lovely hair.' He nuzzled my cheek. 'What are you scowling about now?' He turned my chin towards him.

'Nick, what are you *doing* here?'

He began to laugh. 'We-ell — '

'Oh, don't be an idiot. I'm serious.'

'Perfectly simple. Tour's over. Finished on the 31st January, to be exact.'

'And when do you — go back?'

'To Minzanda? Not at all.'

'Then what *will* you do?'

'That, my love, depends on you. What would you like to do? I've got six months' paid leave and a few shekels put by for us to live on while we think about it, and if you'd rather stay in England — Britain anyway — there's a friend of my father's I can go in with right now in Edinburgh. If you'd like that?'

A friend of his father's. How little, I reflected, I knew about the man I loved. I murmured, 'M'm,' dreamily.

'Or we could have a look at Australia — '

'M'mm.'

'Or there's a post in South Africa that I think I could land if — Hey.' He shook me gently.

'Are you going to say 'M'mm' to everything?'

'M'mm.'

The glint appeared in his eyes. 'Oh, well, in that case — ' I rose hurriedly and picked up the tray.

'That settee makes a good bed, and

I've got stacks of pillows and blankets.'

'I shall sally forth on Monday morning,' he remarked to nobody in particular, 'and set about getting a special licence.'

'That's what all the best seducers say. Besides, who was questioning my virtue a while ago?'

'Ah. That's different. That's when it applies to someone else. And if you think I travelled nearly seven thousand miles and stood outside your door for hours on end in freezing February rain only to let you start dictating terms, you're mad, my girl; that's what.'

We looked at each other for a moment in silence, all our defences down. 'Well,' he said at last. 'Someone's got to be boss. And it'd better be me; I'm bigger.' He put out a hand imperiously.

'So put that tray down again, and come over here.' I hesitated. 'Please, darling?'

I went.

We do hope that you have enjoyed reading this large print book.

Did you know that all of our titles are available for purchase?

We publish a wide range of high quality large print books including:
Romances, Mysteries, Classics
General Fiction
Non Fiction and Westerns

Special interest titles available in large print are:
The Little Oxford Dictionary
Music Book, Song Book
Hymn Book, Service Book

Also available from us courtesy of Oxford University Press:
Young Readers' Dictionary
(large print edition)
Young Readers' Thesaurus
(large print edition)

For further information or a free brochure, please contact us at:
Ulverscroft Large Print Books Ltd.,
The Green, Bradgate Road, Anstey,
Leicester, LE7 7FU, England.
Tel: (00 44) **0116 236 4325**
Fax: (00 44) **0116 234 0205**

Other titles in the
Linford Romance Library:

DUET IN LOW KEY

Doris Rae

In their quiet Highland village, the minister, David Sinclair, and his wife Morag, await the return of their daughter Bridget from convalescence. But a newcomer to the village causes Morag some consternation. Ledoux, big and flamboyant, is a Canadian forester, and has caused a stir locally. Morag fears that Ledoux, at a loose end in the quiet community, might make a play for their gentle and innocent daughter — and the potential for scandal would never do . . .

ONLY A DAY AWAY

Chrissie Loveday

When Sally is offered a position in New Zealand, she sees it as the opportunity of a lifetime. Unfortunately, her mother doesn't share her view — and neither does her fiancé. Sadly, she hands back his ring and looks to an uncertain future. When Adam arrives in her life though, along with a gorgeous little boy, everything becomes even more complicated. But New Zealand works its own brand of magic, and for Sally an unexpected, whole new life is beginning . . .

WHENEVER YOU ARE NEAR

Jeanrose Buczynski

After her break up from a disastrous engagement, Sienna Churchill is ready to make the most of life again and flies to Spain to work as a travel rep with a friend. However, six months later she returns home to her father's farm — and makes a shocking discovery when a ghost from the past reappears . . .

YESTERDAY'S SECRETS

Janet Thomas

Recently divorced archaeologist Jo Kingston comes home to Cornwall with her daughter Sophie to live with her father. When her old 'flame', Nick Angove, is injured on a dig Jo takes over, but faces fierce resentment from him. Then, intriguingly, human bones are found and the police become involved. Nick is injured, apparently when disobeying orders, but actually in saving Sophie's life. And as the truth emerges, they begin to acknowledge that their former love has never really died.

BETHANY'S JUSTICE

Valerie Holmes

When Bethany walks with her friend, Kezzie, to the neighbouring fair, she has no way of knowing that their journey will lead to peril and humiliation. Her friend's infatuation with Bill Judd nearly causes the fall of both young women. Abandoned by Kezzie, Bethany has no notion that the road she now treads will lead her beyond the reach of a family like the Judd's and into the lives of Richard and Bartholomew; who are two very different brothers.

SAPPHIRE IN THE SAND

Patricia Robins

Emma is sixteen years old and in love with Andrew, but he's engaged to Julie, Emma's beautiful elder sister. When their two families go to France on holiday together Emma is perturbed by Julie's casual attitude to the engagement and her interest in Yves Courtelle, another guest at the hotel. Emotions become hopelessly entangled, and for the four young people, the holiday threatens to end in tragedy as they struggle with feelings which are stronger than they are.